"This Co_____ ___ ____ __ Nowhere. My Business Is With Damon's Grandfather. Please Take Me To Him."

"Not until you agree to my proposal," Philip said.

"What proposal?" Ginny snapped. "So far, all I've heard is you pontificating about things you know nothing about."

"Damon's grandfather Jason and I have discussed this, and we've agreed that we will say that you've brought the boy to see me."

"You!" Ginny's eyes widened as a powerful flood of tangled emotions twisted through her. Pretend that she had been Philip Lysander's lover? That she had lain against his naked body? That he had kissed her and… Ginny swallowed against the sudden dryness in her mouth.

"That way, people will assume that the boy—"

"Damon," Ginny corrected. "His name is Damon."

"—is mine."

Dear Reader,

This month: strong and sexy heroes!

First, the Tallchiefs—that intriguing, legendary family—are back, and this time it's Birk Tallchief who meets his match in Cait London's MAN OF THE MONTH, *The Groom Candidate*. Birk's been pining for Lacey MacCandliss for years, but once he gets her, there's nothing but trouble of the most *romantic* kind. Don't miss this delightful story from one of Desire's most beloved writers.

Next, nobody creates a strong, sexy hero quite like Sara Orwig, and in her latest, *Babes in Arms,* she brings us Colin Whitefeather, a tough and tender man you'll never forget. And in Judith McWilliams's *Another Man's Baby* we meet Philip Lysander, a Greek tycoon who will do anything to save his family...even pretend to be a child's father.

Peggy Moreland's delightful miniseries, TROUBLE IN TEXAS, continues with *Lone Star Kind of Man*. The man in question is rugged rogue cowboy Cody Fipes. In *Big Sky Drifter,* by Doreen Owens Malek, a wild Wyoming man named Cal Winston tames a lonely woman. And in Cathie Linz's *Husband Needed,* bachelor Jack Elliott surprises himself when he offers to trade his single days for married nights.

In Silhouette Desire you'll always find the most irresistible men around! So enjoy!

Lucia Macro

Senior Editor

Please address questions and book requests to:
Silhouette Reader Service
U.S.: 3010 Walden Ave., P.O. Box 1325, Buffalo, NY 14269
Canadian: P.O. Box 609, Fort Erie, Ont. L2A 5X3

JUDITH McWILLIAMS
ANOTHER MAN'S BABY

SILHOUETTE *Desire*®
Published by Silhouette Books
America's Publisher of Contemporary Romance

If you purchased this book without a cover you should be aware
that this book is stolen property. It was reported as "unsold and
destroyed" to the publisher, and neither the author nor the
publisher has received any payment for this "stripped book."

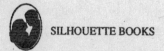

SILHOUETTE BOOKS

ISBN 0-373-76095-7

ANOTHER MAN'S BABY

Copyright © 1997 by Judith McWilliams

All rights reserved. Except for use in any review, the reproduction
or utilization of this work in whole or in part in any form by any
electronic, mechanical or other means, now known or hereafter
invented, including xerography, photocopying and recording, or in
any information storage or retrieval system, is forbidden without
the written permission of the editorial office, Silhouette Books,
300 East 42nd Street, New York, NY 10017 U.S.A.

All characters in this book have no existence outside the imagination of
the author and have no relation whatsoever to anyone bearing the same
name or names. They are not even distantly inspired by any individual
known or unknown to the author, and all incidents are pure invention.

This edition published by arrangement with Harlequin Books S.A.

® and TM are trademarks of Harlequin Books S.A., used under license.
Trademarks indicated with ® are registered in the United States Patent
and Trademark Office, the Canadian Trade Marks Office and in other
countries.

Printed in U.S.A.

Books by Judith McWilliams

Silhouette Desire

Reluctant Partners #441
A Perfect Season #545
That's My Baby #597
Anything's Possible! #911
The Man from Atlantis #954
Instant Husband #1001
Practice Husband #1062
Another Man's Baby #1095

Silhouette Romance

Gift of the Gods #479

JUDITH McWILLIAMS

began to enjoy romances while in search of the prover-
bial "happily ever afters." But she always found
herself rewriting the endings, and eventually the
beginnings, of the books she read. Then her husband
finally suggested that she write novels of her own, and
she's been doing so ever since. An ex-teacher with
four children, Judith has traveled the country extensively with her husband and has been greatly
influenced by those experiences. But while not tending
the garden or caring for family, Judith does what she
enjoys most—writing. She has also written under the
name Charlotte Hines.

Prologue

"**W**hat happened? Why aren't you at work? It's two o'clock."

Reluctantly, Ginny Alton turned as the whiny sound of her next-door neighbor's voice accosted her.

"Good afternoon, Mrs. Rolle," Ginny said, shifting her heavy bag of groceries from one slim hip to the other.

"Not so far it hasn't been." Mrs. Rolle's voice took on a peevish note that Ginny very much feared was a prelude to a recital of her problems, real and imaginary. Normally, Ginny listened patiently to the elderly woman's seemingly inexhaustible supply of complaints because she felt sorry for her, but today she simply didn't have the time.

"That's too bad," Ginny murmured as she inched closer to her apartment door. "But I really can't stop to talk. My cousin is waiting for the baby's formula." She knocked softly on the door, not wanting to wake up Damon if he were sleeping.

"Has Beth given you cancer, too? Is that why you're not at work?" Mrs. Rolle's face took on an avid expression that chilled Ginny.

"Leukemia is not contagious." Ginny knocked again, a little harder this time, mentally urging Beth to hurry before she said something very rude.

"Ha! What do doctors know? Why, when they took out my gall bladder—"

Ginny ignored the oft-repeated story as she fished her key out of the pocket of her well-worn jeans. Why hadn't Beth answered? she wondered uneasily. She wasn't strong enough to leave the apartment by herself. Could she have had a delayed reaction to yesterday's chemotherapy treatment? Could she have fainted?

An escalating sense of urgency filled Ginny as she unlocked the door and shoved it open. Dropping the groceries just inside, she closed the door behind her, not even hearing Mrs. Rolle's outraged gasp.

Fearfully, Ginny glanced around her spacious living room, but it was empty. As was the small kitchen with its minuscule dining area. Ginny was about to check the bedroom Beth shared with her son when the muffled sound of sobbing raised the hair on the back of her neck.

Ginny hurried down the hall toward the heartbroken sound. It was coming from her own bedroom. Ginny silently pushed the door open and found Beth sitting in the middle of her bed crying in a hopeless fashion that tore at Ginny's heart.

"Hey, it's not that bad, kiddo." Ginny made a determined effort to sound positive. "You know the doctor says that by this time next year you'll be back in the classroom with your kindergartners. Although why he would want to threaten you with that..."

Beth didn't smile as Ginny had hoped. She merely

sobbed all the harder. As if... A cold slither of fear trickled through Ginny. Could the hospital have called with bad news while she had been out doing their grocery shopping?

"Beth, tell me what happened." Ginny fought to keep her panic out of her voice. Beth was hard-pressed to deal with her own fears. She certainly couldn't deal with Ginny's, too.

Beth looked up, and her bleak, lost expression made Ginny want to sit down and cry with her.

"He...he said I was lying. He said..." Her voice dissolved into tears.

"He who?"

Beth fumbled behind her and picked up a crumpled sheet of paper that she waved at Ginny. "Creon's father. He said that I'm lying. That Damon couldn't be Creon's son. That Creon would never have had an affair with me. That I'm only saying it now because Creon's dead and can't defend himself. He said...that Creon would never have been capable of loving someone like me," Beth finished on a rush.

Ginny clenched her teeth to keep from blurting out just what she thought that jerk Creon had been capable of. It would only upset Beth further because she was totally blind where Creon was concerned. Even after he had deserted her to return to his native Greece, Beth had believed that he really loved her and would eventually return and marry her and that they and their child would live happily ever after. Despite all evidence to the contrary, she had continued to believe it right up until Creon had managed to get himself killed in a speedboat accident six months ago.

"Let me see that." Ginny took the letter out of Beth's hot fingers and quickly scanned it. Her sense of anger grew with every word she read.

"Damon is his grandson. Why won't Mr. Papas admit

it?'' Beth's lower lip quivered piteously. ''All I'm asking him to do is to provide for his education.

''Normally, I wouldn't even care about his school fees, but if I die...'' Beth's voice faltered.

''You aren't going to die!'' Ginny said emphatically, as if the very force of her denial could make it so. ''The doctor says you have every chance of making a complete recovery.''

''But there's still a chance that I won't get better,'' Beth persisted. ''And if I don't, I won't be here to tell Damon about his father and how much he loved me and how glad he was when he found out I was pregnant and how he wanted to marry me, but he couldn't until his father got over his heart attack.'' Beth gulped back more tears.

Ginny shoved her fingers through her shoulder-length blond hair in frustration. It seemed as if the sicker Beth got, the more important it became to her to force Jason Papas to acknowledge his grandson. It preyed on Beth's mind, using up precious emotional energy that she needed to fight the cancer threatening her life.

Ginny looked back down at the letter, frowning when she realized that this was only the first page.

''Where's the rest of this?'' she asked Beth.

Beth peered around and found the second sheet on the floor beside the bed. Picking it up, she handed it to Ginny.

Ginny's deep blue eyes darkened incredulously as she read it. ''After calling you an opportunistic liar, he wants you and Damon to fly to Greece and discuss the matter with him!''

Beth nodded. ''There was a pair of plane tickets included. Funny, isn't it? I can't even walk to the corner store, and I'm supposed to fly to Greece with a four-month-old baby. I guess I should have told him about my being sick, but I didn't want it to seem as if... And now I can't..." Beth paused and her eyes suddenly focused on Ginny. "But you can," she said slowly.

"Me! Why would I want to see this—" Ginny gestured impotently with the letter "—this parody of a human being?"

"Ginny, listen." Beth grabbed hold of Ginny's long slender fingers and held on to them as if they were a lifeline. "You could go, pretending to be me. Damon would be perfectly happy with you, and you're very good with him. And I never used my first name when I wrote to Creon's father." Beth rushed on when Ginny opened her mouth. "All Jason Papas knows me by is Miss Alton. And you're Miss Alton, too. I wouldn't ask you, but I'm so worried about Damon's future if I should..."

"Beth, I swear to you. I'll take care of Damon, no matter what happens," Ginny vowed.

"Yes, but what about when you marry? Will your husband want to spend money on your dead cousin's orphan?"

"You always did have an overactive imagination," Ginny said dryly. "I'm not even dating anyone, let alone considering marriage to a miser."

"Wait till you fall in love," Beth said sadly. "You won't even notice that he's cheap."

Like you never noticed that Creon Papas was an immature jerk, Ginny thought on a wave of guilt. If she hadn't brought him to the apartment, Beth would never have met him and never had an affair with him and never had been left holding a baby. Literally.

Ginny absently chewed on her lower lip as she tried to rationally consider Beth's idea. She didn't like it, but she had to admit that Beth was right about one thing. It was feasible. Since the investment firm where Ginny worked was allowing her to work at home while Beth was undergoing chemotherapy, she was free to go to Greece.

Not only that, but mentally she was far better equipped to deal with a tyrant like Jason Papas than the shy, retiring Beth was. Jason Papas wouldn't be able to browbeat her. One thing her career as an financial analyst had taught her was how to stand up to male chauvinists and petty bullies. And much as she disliked lying about who and what she was, she liked the alternative of Beth brooding about the situation even less.

And it wasn't as if she were going to personally gain anything by impersonating Beth, Ginny rationalized. All Beth wanted from the very wealthy Jason Papas was for him to provide for his grandson's education.

That and to acknowledge that Damon had a right to the Papas family's support. An acknowledgment that Ginny suspected was far more important to Beth than the money.

Ginny let her breath out on a long, shuddering sigh. Despite her doubts about the wisdom of the impersonation, she couldn't see any way to refuse Beth's request. Beth needed to forge some kind of relationship with Creon's family. Needed it to relieve her mind so that she could concentrate on getting better.

"All right, I'll do it," Ginny said, and then shivered as her words seemed to hang ominously in the air like a portent of disaster to come.

One

Ginny looked around the airport lounge where Jason Papas's letter had told Beth she'd be met. It was deserted. Ginny sighed. Of course Jason Papas hadn't bothered to show up. It was entirely in keeping with the rest of her trip. A disaster from start to finish. If there was anything worse than taking a long plane trip with a four-month-old baby, she didn't want to find out about it.

Being extremely careful not to wake the now-sleeping Damon, Ginny set his car seat down on the floor. To her relief, he didn't stir.

Wearily she sank down in a seat and checked her watch. Ten-fifteen. Only thirty-five minutes past the time her flight had been scheduled to arrive. Not very late for a flight that had originated in New York.

Where was Jason Papas? Ginny wondered, as annoyance began to nudge aside her tiredness. Damon needed to be changed and fed and put into a proper bed. And she needed a shower. Ginny glanced in distaste at her rumpled blue linen suit with its varied collection of baby stains garnered in the course of the long trip.

Could leaving her cooling her heels here at the airport be a deliberate tactic on Jason Papas's part? A tactic designed to impress on her the fact that he didn't think neither she nor Damon was important enough to be met on time?

It was certainly possible. In fact, if Jason Papas was anything like his obnoxious son then it was probable. But while those kinds of tactics would have reduced the gentle Beth to a dithering mass of uncertainty, they only made Ginny mad. And more determined than ever to stand up to the old tyrant.

Absently, Ginny brushed back a strand of hair that had escaped from her chignon. She'd wait another fifteen minutes on the off chance that Jason Papas's delay had been caused by traffic, and then she'd leave a message for him at the airline desk and check into a hotel.

Feeling slightly better now that she'd decided on a plan of action, Ginny leaned her head back against the seat and closed her eyes. Within seconds she was asleep.

Philip Lysander pushed back the sleeve of his gray suit jacket and looked down at the thin gold watch on his wrist. He'd kept this Alton woman and the bastard she was trying to trick a sick old man into acknowledging waiting forty minutes now. Long enough to drive home the fact to her that the family considered her entirely insignificant. It was now time to pick her up.

Draining the remainder of his whiskey, Philip set the empty glass back down on the table and left the airport's bar.

It took him five minutes to locate the lounge where Jason had told him the Alton woman would be waiting. Philip had absolutely no doubt that she would be there. Anyone brazen enough to try to pull off the fraud she was attempting wouldn't back out at the last minute.

Despite having his opinion confirmed, Philip took no satisfaction from the sight of the woman sitting on the far side of the lounge with a car seat at her feet. He headed toward her, relishing the prospect of telling her that she wasn't going to get away with her lie. That he knew her for what she was and would never allow her to harm his family.

His lips tightened when he realized that she was asleep. It seemed the final insult to him that she should be blissfully unaware of the fact that he'd kept her waiting.

Philip's eyes widened in surprise as he got close enough to get a good look at the woman. Instead of the cheap, overblown opportunist that he'd been expecting, she looked...elegant, he finally settled on. Her dark blond hair was the exact shade of the lemon blossom honey his mother used to pour on his breakfast toast when he'd been a child. It even looked like honey, sleek and smooth. Unconsciously his fingers twitched with the urge to stroke her hair and see if it were as silky as it looked.

His gaze wandered lower, down over her face, and his mouth dried under the impact of her beauty. And she was beautiful, Philip reluctantly conceded. Not only did she have classically perfect features, but a flawless complexion, as well. His eyes lingered on the pale rose flush on her cheekbones before dropping down to the soft lusciousness of her full mouth. He swallowed uneasily as an unexpected urge to press his own mouth to hers slammed through him.

He wrenched his gaze away from the lure of her lips with effort, focusing instead on the slight swell of her breasts beneath the severely cut blue suit she was wearing. He frowned at her outfit. It didn't fit her delectable body.

Someone as feminine as she looked should be wearing something soft and clinging and...

He pulled his imagination up short. What was the matter with him? he wondered uneasily. He wasn't some immature boy to be thrown off balance by the sight of a woman's body, no matter how beautiful it was. Especially not when he knew that the character behind the beautiful facade was rotten to the core. His features hardened. He couldn't afford to forget for a moment what she was really like.

Ginny stirred uneasily as a prickly sensation danced over her skin. Confused, she half opened her eyes and checked Damon. He was still sleeping. A soft smile curved her lips at his peaceful expression. She started to yawn and then stopped as she caught sight of a pair of gray-covered legs standing slightly behind Damon's car seat.

Dreamily, her eyes followed the pants upward over a powerful pair of masculine thighs, up over a flat stomach to a broad chest. Approvingly, she noted the impressive breadth of his shoulders, but she wasn't so sure about the hard thrust of his jaw. He looked very determined. Ginny watched his long tanned fingers clench spasmodically. His fingers should be wrapped around a spear, she thought whimsically. And instead of a suit, he should be wearing one of those short white skirt things the ancient Spartan warriors wore. No, even better, he should be an athlete. Her stomach twisted in instinctive response to the sudden image she had of him naked. His bare skin was gleaming with the oil that the athletes rubbed on it and...

An icy sensation suddenly ripped through her languid daydreams as her eyes collided with his coal black ones. They seemed to smolder with suppressed emotion. An impression heightened by his tightly compressed lips.

Ginny slowly straightened up, trying not to let him see

just how disoriented she was. She'd only found him fascinating because she was so tired, she assured herself. Tired and half-asleep. Under normal circumstances this was not a man who would appeal to her, not for a second. As she quite obviously didn't appeal to him. She watched the imperious way he was regarding her. As if she were a bad smell that he intended to eliminate as soon as possible.

He couldn't possibly be Jason Papas. He was far too young. So it stood to reason that he was an emissary of Jason Papas sent to pick her and Damon up like a stray package that had to be dealt with.

Ginny was unable to entirely suppress her feeling of unease as the man's features hardened even further, reminding her of a painting she'd once seen of a judge at the Salem witch trials. He looked absolutely merciless. But she didn't want mercy, she bolstered her sagging courage. She wanted justice. Justice for Damon and poor Beth. And this man, no matter who he was, wasn't going to stop her!

Ginny squared her shoulders and returned his glare, waiting for him to break the brittle silence that stretched between them.

Finally, just when she was starting to feel limp with the strain, he did.

"You won't get away with it!" His intriguingly accented voice was rasped seductively over her nerve endings.

"And what precisely is 'it'? For that matter, who are you?"

"I'm here to pick you up." His voice held a sneer that seemed to insinuate all kinds of things.

Ginny ignored it and simply stared at him, waiting for him to answer her question. Experience had taught her that it was fatal to try to placate men like him. They had to be met with determination.

"Well! Have you nothing to say?"

"I'm still waiting for you to tell me who you are," she managed a level tone despite the butterflies holding a convention in her stomach. "Or isn't your command of the English language sufficient to have understood my question?"

Ginny felt a brief flair of satisfaction as his tanned cheeks darkened at her gibe.

"I have a degree in economics from Oxford, and I spend most of my time in London!" he snapped.

"Lovely." Ginny gave him a bland smile. "But that still doesn't tell me who you are."

"Philip Lysander, Creon's brother-in-law. He was married to my sister, Lydia."

"Brother-in-law!" Ginny stared blankly at him as a dizzying wave of horror washed over her. Creon had been married! He was even worse than she'd thought, and she hadn't thought all that much of him in the first place.

Philip's smile chilled her. "Creon may be dead and unable to defend himself from your lies, but he has family who will."

And so did Beth, Ginny thought grimly. As Creon's precious family would find out.

"All right, Philip Lysander, Creon's brother-in-law. How about if you do what you were sent to do and take me to Jason Papas."

"Not until we reach an agreement."

Ginny eyed him warily. "About what?"

"I don't want my sister hurt."

Ginny felt a spurt of sympathy for the unknown Lydia, but she determinedly banished it. Philip's sister had him and her father-in-law and heaven only knew how many other relatives to help her cope with the situation. Poor Beth only had her to depend on, and Ginny had no intention of failing her.

"You want Jason Papas to sacrifice his grandson so that your sister won't have to face the type of man she married?"

"The boy isn't Creon's son, and you know it!"

Ginny sighed, suddenly feeling tired to the point of numbness. "This conversation is getting us nowhere. My business is with Damon's grandfather. Please take me to him."

"Not until you agree to my proposal."

"What proposal?" she snapped. "So far all I've heard is you pontificating about things you know nothing about."

"Jason and I have discussed this, and we've agreed that we will say that you've brought the boy to Greece to see me."

"You!" Ginny's eyes widened as a powerful flood of tangled emotions twisted through her. Pretend that she had been Philip Lysander's lover? That she had lain against his naked body? That he had kissed her and... Ginny swallowed against the sudden dryness in her mouth.

"That way people will assume that the boy—"

"Damon," Ginny corrected. "His name is Damon."

Philip ignored her. "...is mine, and Lydia will be protected from gossip."

"No!" Ginny's instinctive denial seemed to echo around them. She didn't want to be close to this man. To even pretend to be close. He made her feel very unlike herself, and until she was absolutely certain that her unusual reaction to him was caused by tiredness and worry about Damon and Beth, she didn't want to risk further exposure to him.

"No," she repeated in a level tone of voice.

"Then I won't take you to see Jason." Philip gave her a smug look that made her want to smack him—hard—and that worried her almost as much as her body's strange re-

sponse to him. She was not a violent person. She had nothing but contempt for people who thought that violence was
an acceptable form of self-expression.

But thinking about hitting him was not the same thing
as doing it, she rationalized. Thinking about it was nothing
more than a safety valve for explosive feelings.

Making a valiant attempt to block Philip out of her mind,
Ginny stared down at the floor at her feet and tried to think.
Despite her best efforts back in New York, she had been
unable to locate Jason Papas's home address. Even Beth
had had to send her letter to his company's headquarters
here in Athens. And while she could visit his company, she
very much doubted that his employees would be willing to
tell her, without his consent, where to find him.

So if she refused to go along with Philip's charade, then
her chances of locating Jason weren't good. And her trip
to Greece would have been a waste of time. Ginny winced
at the thought of having to go back to Beth and tell her
that she hadn't even been able to speak to Jason.

Having come so far, she couldn't fail Beth now. And it
wasn't as if she were some young, naive fool to be over-
awed by a sophisticated man of the world like Philip Lysander obviously was. She was a highly intelligent, experienced, professional woman of thirty-two. She could cope
with him. Even if her weird reaction to him didn't fade
after a good night's sleep, she could still cope.

"Very well." Ginny got to her feet. "I will allow the
masquerade to stand, but I refuse to tell a direct lie to anyone about who Damon's father is."

Philip gave her a scathing look. "Spare me the claim to
ethics."

"I'd just as soon spare you, period! Having anything to
do with you wasn't my idea."

To Ginny's shock, Philip suddenly grabbed her and

yanked her up against him. She hit his chest with a thump.
It was like hitting a wall—hard, with no give whatsoever.
Ginny took a deep breath to ask him just what he thought
he was doing, but it proved to be a mistake. Her lungs were
immediately inundated with the subtle scent of a men's
cologne that made her think of soldiers and horses and...

"Stop it," she muttered, not sure if she was talking to
her own wayward body or to him. Both of them ignored
her.

His arms tightened around her, molding her slender
frame to his hard curves and making her excruciatingly
aware of the basic differences between their bodies.

Ginny looked up at him, and he quickly took advantage
of her movement to capture her mouth. His lips were warm
and pliable as they pressed against hers. His tongue darted
out to lick her bottom lip, and Ginny shivered violently at
the sensation.

The urge to open her mouth was overwhelming, but it
was the very intensity of her reaction that set off alarm
bells deep in her mind. Shoving her hands between them,
she tried to push him back, but he didn't budge. She tried
to wiggle out of his arms, but the sharp prickles of pleasure
that tore through her as her breasts scraped across his chest
distracted her, and he took advantage of her hesitation to
bind her even closer to him.

Ginny could see lights flickering behind her closed eyelids as if her exploding emotions were finding a physical
release. Lights that... Flashbulbs! She suddenly identified
the lights. Someone was taking pictures.

Her eyes shot open, and she found herself staring into
Philip's gleaming black eyes. Wrenching her gaze away,
she saw a thin man with a large, professional-looking cam-
era hurrying away from them.

"Who was that, and why did you kiss me?" she demanded, operating under the old adage that a good offense is the best defense.

"One of the paparazzi who hang around the airport and take pictures they hope to sell to the scandal sheets."

And he'd kissed her to give added weight to the lie that he was her lover and Damon's father, Ginny realized in dismay. What had she gotten herself into?

Suddenly realizing that she was still pressed up against Philip's warm body, Ginny hastily stepped back and stumbled over her purse, which was sitting on the floor.

Philip grabbed her, steadying her for a moment against his hard frame. It was long enough for her body to react with a growing sense of urgency.

Desperately, Ginny tore herself out of his grip.

"I'm tired after that long flight." She muttered the first excuse that came to mind.

"Next time, pick a victim a little closer to home!" Philip snapped as he bent to pick up Damon's car seat.

As he lifted it, the blanket that had been partially obscuring the child's face fell back, and an uneasy feeling washed over Philip as he got his first clear look at the child. The boy had the same inky black hair and dark complexion that Creon had had. As he did himself, Philip reminded himself. There were millions of men with dark hair and dark complexions in Greece. That didn't prove anything.

"Come on," he flung at Ginny as he headed toward the doors.

"What about my luggage?" Ginny hurried to match his long stride. "And don't swing that car seat around." Her voice sharpened. "I don't want Damon to wake up."

"I had a porter fetch your luggage and put it in my car."

So she'd been right. He had deliberately left her waiting, Ginny thought in annoyance.

Knowing that nothing she could say about his unconscionable behavior would bother him, she wisely said nothing, contenting herself with glaring at his broad back as he marched out the door.

She wasn't the least bit surprised to find his car parked in a no-parking zone. Nor was she surprised to find that no one had done anything about it. Philip was clearly the type of man it wasn't safe to cross. But someone should have done so long ago, she thought grimly. He'd have developed into a much nicer person if he'd been thwarted occasionally.

Well, it was never too late for him to learn and, while it wasn't a job Ginny would have normally chosen, she was fast coming to the conclusion that she would be doing her fellow man a distinct service if she were to teach Philip that the whole world didn't dance to his piping.

Ginny surreptitiously watched Philip while she carefully buckled Damon's car seat into the back seat of his black Mercedes. He was sitting in the driver's seat looking at something on the console between the two front seats. There was an absorbed expression on his lean face that bespoke total concentration.

Was he married? Ginny wondered as she studied the slight frown between his dark eyebrows. A sudden urge to smooth the worry line away gripped her and, shaken by the impulse, she turned back to Damon. She didn't understand her almost compulsive physical attraction to Philip. She was far more aware of him than she had ever been of any male, and that was on the basis of a half hour's acquaintance. Even, Ted whom she'd seriously considered marrying a few years ago, hadn't affected her like this. But why? The question reverberated through her tired mind, demanding an answer.

Probably because of the intense emotions behind their meeting, she rationalized. And when she added to that the fact that she was exhausted, it was no wonder that she was acting out of character. With any luck at all, she'd be back to normal by morning and she'd be able to see Philip as nothing more than the ruggedly handsome, gorgeously built, smugly self-righteous man he was. Till then, she'd simply have to be careful not to do or say anything to let him guess just what she was feeling, because one thing she'd bet her last dollar on was that Philip was a man who would ruthlessly exploit any advantage he could get.

Dropping a gentle kiss on Damon's petal-soft cheek, Ginny got into the front seat.

"Buckle your seat belt," Philip ordered.

Ginny blinked and reached for the ends of the belt. She really was tired, she thought ruefully, to have forgotten something that basic.

"A miracle," Philip muttered as he pulled away from the curb. "She actually did as she was told without an argument."

Ginny ignored the comment. She had the disheartening feeling that she was going to be ignoring a lot of things in the next few days.

"Where does Damon's grandfather live?" she asked as Philip wound his way through the brilliantly lit streets of Athens.

"I have no idea," he shot back, "but Jason Papas lives in Glifadha, but we aren't going there tonight."

Ginny froze as, for one mad second, images of being driven into the hinterlands and abandoned filled her mind. No, she assured herself. Creon might have been selfish enough to have tried that type of intimidation, but she didn't think that was Philip's style.

"Then where are we going?" Ginny was pleased at the evenness of her tone.

"My apartment." He accelerated around a slow-moving tourist bus and then turned left in front of a speeding taxi.

Ginny gasped and cast a worried look over her shoulder at Damon. He was still sleeping peacefully. "I can see why you want your passengers to wear seat belts," she muttered. "You have a death wish."

Philip gave her a quick grin that sent an unexpected rush of pleasure through her. For one moment, he had looked young and carefree and someone she...

Stop it! Ginny hastily pulled her imagination up short because that was all it was. Imagination. She absolutely couldn't fall into the trap of assuming Philip had the qualities she wanted him to have.

"Let me guess," she said dryly. "You have an etching you want to show me?"

Philip looked confused. "The only etchings I have are four by da Vinci, and they're in my London house."

Ginny stared at him, mentally revising her estimation of his wealth upward by quite a few million. Da Vincis were not cheap and for him to own four...

"Are you an art lover, besides a blackmailer?" he asked.

Ginny determinedly ignored the slur. Hopefully, if she refused to respond to his provocation, he'd lose interest in baiting her. "Sorry, I forgot you were a foreigner and wouldn't know that 'looking at etchings' is an American expression."

"I am not a foreigner. I am Greek, this is Greece. Therefore, you are the foreigner."

"Great," she muttered. "Just what I need. A literalist."

"And what does inviting someone to see your etching mean?" he persisted.

Ginny stared into his face, watching the way the light from a pink neon restaurant sign engulfed him in a colorful glow. Could he really not have run across the expression before? But it didn't really matter because if she refused to answer him, he'd realize that she found discussing sex with him unsettling. And no doubt use the information to torment her at some future date. Her only viable option at this point would be to act nonchalant. Or at least try.

"It means that a man is asking a woman to his apartment in the hopes of convincing her to have sex with him," she finally said.

"Have sex?" He shot her a quick, calculating glance that made her very leery. "And would you have sex with me, Ginny Alton? Would you let me kiss you the way a lover kisses a woman? Would you let me strip that sterile-looking suit off you? Would you let me take your breasts in my hands and explore their texture? Would you let me kiss your breasts and suckle—"

"Stop it!" Ginny choked out, giving up trying to ignore him. Philip was treating her as he would a woman that he'd picked up for one purpose and one purpose only, and she wasn't going to allow it.

He momentarily took his eyes off the road to glance at her flushed face. He could almost believe she was embarrassed, but that made no sense. His words hadn't been all that explicit. Certainly not explicit enough to make a blackmailer with an illegitimate child blush. So why had she? He didn't know but he fully intended to find out. By the time he was through with Ginny Alton she wouldn't have a secret left.

"Or...or I'll tell your wife," Ginny finally threatened.

He chuckled. "I have no wife. You could always threaten to tell my mother, not that you're likely to meet her. I try to protect her from the seamier side of life."

Ginny ignored the insult as well as the strange spurt of pleasure she felt at his bachelor state. Instead, she turned her head and stared out the car window at the quiet, residential neighborhood he was driving through. Closing her eyes, she tried to employ one of the relaxation techniques she'd learned to use when her clients were being more exasperating than usual.

As it was in the beginning, is now and ever will be, she doggedly repeated to herself. But instead of evoking a feeling of peace as it was supposed to, all she could think about was how perfectly it appeared to describe Philip's flat refusal to even consider the truth of what she was saying. But why wouldn't he consider it? she wondered. Granted, he wanted to protect his sister, but hiding the truth from her wasn't much protection.

For that matter, why hadn't he stopped his sister from marrying Creon in the first place? It had only taken her one date to realize that Creon was bad news. Philip should have been able to figure it out, too.

Maybe because Philip didn't see anything wrong with a man carrying on affairs on the side as long as his wife didn't find out about it? She found the idea depressing.

"You get the boy."

Ginny looked around, realizing that Philip had parked the car in front of a tall, ultramodern apartment building. It looked expensive, exclusive and totally unwelcoming. As if it were nothing more than a stage prop. She wouldn't want to live there. But then she wasn't being asked to, she reminded herself as she scrambled out of the car.

Ginny bumped Damon's car seat against the front seat as she was pulling it out of the car. The jolt woke the baby, and he glared at her, for one eerie moment looking exactly like Philip.

"Don't do that, love." She gave him a kiss.

Damon was not soothed. He opened his small mouth and emitted a bellow that could be heard for a block in either direction.

"Ah, he must be a boy with lungs like that." The doorman nodded approvingly at Damon as he opened the lobby door for them. Ginny ignored the man.

"Don't cry, sweet'n. Just as soon as we get inside, I'll give you a bottle."

Damon stuck out his lower lip as if considering whether or not to accept her offer.

Philip handed the doorman his car keys. "Have someone bring the luggage in the trunk." He started toward the bank of elevators.

Ginny trailed after Philip, trying to ignore the speculative stares she was getting from the people in the lobby. She breathed a sigh of relief when the elevator doors finally opened, but her relief didn't last long. A young woman wearing five-inch heels and a superbly cut, slinky black sheath dress hurried into the elevator after them.

"Why, Philip, I didn't know you were back in Greece. Who's this?" The woman gestured toward Ginny.

To Ginny's shock, Philip put his arm around her waist and pulled her up against his hard side. She could feel him pressing into her hip and the heat from his body was crowding her, forcing her out of her comfort zones. But she wasn't the only one disconcerted by Philip's actions, Ginny realized, when she saw the incredulous look on the woman's face.

"This is Ginny Alton." Philip's voice deepened as if with a hint of some deeply held emotion. "Ginny, this is Thera Spirios, an old friend of my sister Clytie."

"Not Clytie, Philip. Sophie." The woman's features sharpened in annoyance. "Clytie is years older than me."

"I'm pleased to meet you," Ginny lied.

The woman nodded impatiently at Ginny and turned back to Philip. "You are coming to the reception at the French embassy this evening, aren't you, Philip?"

"No." Philip gave Ginny a smoldering look that implied he intended to spend his evening making love to her. Even though Ginny knew the look was strictly for show, it still sent an involuntary shiver of anticipation through her.

Why couldn't Philip have been more like Creon? she thought in dismay. She had had no trouble resisting that philanderer. Why was Philip different?

"Who's that?" Thera peered closer at Damon who reacted to the unfriendly face by shrieking.

To Ginny's relief, the elevator doors slid open before Philip could answer Thera. Not waiting for him, Ginny hurried through them into the spacious hallway beyond.

Philip paused a moment to say something to Thera that Ginny couldn't quite catch. But whatever it was, it didn't sit well with the woman. Her face turned an unbecoming shade of red, and her thin lips twisted as she stared in impotent frustration as Philip walked out of the elevator.

A discarded girlfriend? Ginny wondered, but had better sense than to ask. Instead, she jiggled the wailing Damon as she waited for Philip to unlock his apartment door.

Ginny followed Philip inside, looking around curiously. The apartment was expensively decorated and very spacious, but it was also strangely impersonal. It looked more like a luxury hotel suite than a private home.

Damon's howls increased, and Ginny set his car seat down and struggled to unbuckle his squirming body.

"You're doing that wrong." Philip brushed her fingers away and deftly unfastened the buckles.

"Fine. Since you know so much, you can take care of him while I heat his bottle."

Rather to her surprise, he didn't refuse. Instead, he picked Damon up, holding him out in front of him as if he were a live grenade that might explode at any minute.

"Don't hold him like that," Ginny ordered as she rummaged through Damon's diaper bag for a bottle of formula. "Babies need to feel secure. Where's the kitchen?"

"Through there." He nodded toward the right with his head as he gingerly put Damon on his shoulder. "He squishes!" Philip's eyes widened in horror.

Ginny gave him a limpid smile. "So change him. There's plenty of diapers in the bag."

Grateful that Damon was too young to understand the meaning of some of the words Philip was muttering, Ginny headed toward the kitchen.

It didn't take her long to heat the bottle. She was testing the warmth of the formula on her wrist when she heard Philip bellow. It was immediately followed by Damon's shriek.

For a moment, she was tempted to leave Philip to solve whatever mess he'd managed to get himself into. Or that Damon had managed to create. But she finally decided that poor Damon had had to put up with enough today.

Ginny followed the sound of Damon's crying to a large bedroom that was dominated by a huge bed. She gulped as her skin began to tingle. Grimly she tried to squash the unwanted reaction, but it simply burrowed deeper into her chest, raising all sorts of longings. She felt rattled and uncertain—like an adolescent who'd unexpectedly found herself alone in a bedroom with a boy, and she didn't like the feeling one bit.

"What are you doing?" Her voice was curt with the effort she was making to control her emotions.

Philip raised his head and gave her an agonized look. "The boy..." He gestured from the baby to his chest.

Ginny frowned and then grinned as she suddenly realized what must have happened. When Philip had taken Damon's wet diaper off, the baby had reacted to the room's air-conditioning by urinating. All over the front of Philip. Her lips twitched at the thought of the ultrasophisticated Philip being caught unawares. She tried to swallow her laughter, but a giggle escaped.

"I'm sorry," she choked out with far more politeness than sincerity. "But you..." She completely lost her attempts to control her mirth.

The warm, happy sound of her laughter rolled over Philip's annoyance, vanquishing it. Intrigued, Philip watched the way her soft lips quirked at the corners. He wanted to take her in his arms and press his mouth against her quivering lips. To absorb her laughter into his own body.

If this was the side of her personality that she'd shown to Creon, it was no wonder that he'd... No! Philip emphatically banished the traitorous thought.

"You finish the boy. I'm going to take a shower." He stalked toward his bathroom, angry at himself for even considering that she might be telling the truth. Creon wouldn't have done such a despicable thing to Lydia, and he was dishonoring Creon's memory by even considering the idea.

Philip's abrupt exit successfully stilled Ginny's mirth, and she hurried over to the bed before Damon rolled over and fell off.

"Poor little angel," she murmured soothingly as she deftly diapered him. "Don't you worry. I don't hold it against you. Come on, love. Let's get some food into your tummy and then you can go to sleep."

Picking Damon up, she went back to the living room and, sitting down on the very comfortable sofa, popped the nipple into Damon's mouth. He began to gulp the formula down as if he were in imminent danger of starvation.

Damon polished off his bottle in record time, and Ginny was trying to coax a burp out of him when the phone suddenly rang. She glanced from the phone on the end table to the hallway that led to Philip's bedroom. Was he still in the shower? Would he want her to answer it?

But even if she did answer it, the person calling might not speak English.

"Should I answer it?" Ginny asked Damon, who wrinkled his button nose and then emitted a huge burp. She chuckled and kissed his downy head. "My sentiments exactly. We'll..."

She turned at the muffled sound of footsteps on the thick carpeting behind her.

Two

Ginny tensed as she watched Philip stride across the living room. He was wearing a short, white towel wrapped around his lean waist, and nothing else. She stared at his broad chest in fascination. It was covered with a thick pelt of dark hair that intrigued her. She wanted to run her hands over it and see what it felt like. To find out if it were soft and silky or crisp and abrasive.

Mesmerized, Ginny watched the supple movement of the muscles beneath his tautly stretched skin as he picked up the phone. There wasn't an ounce of fat on him. Anywhere. Her eyes drifted lower, down over his flat hips and strong legs. Her mouth dried as she watched water droplets trickle down his legs. Slowly, enticingly, the drops caressed his flesh as they meandered downward. She wanted to follow their path. To trace over it with her fingertips and then with her lips.

Philip gestured emphatically as he responded to something his caller had said, and Ginny shivered as Philip's towel momentarily parted, giving her a tantalizing glimpse of his masculinity. Her eyelids felt heavy, and a tightness was wrapping itself around her chest, making it difficult to take a deep breath.

This was crazy! She made a valiant effort to regain control of her wayward responses. How could she be sitting here all but drooling over a man that she barely knew, and what little she did know she didn't like? It made no sense.

Ginny tried closing her eyes to shut out the temptation, but it didn't help. She found Philip's powerful body clearly imprinted on the back of her eyelids.

Flustered, she opened her eyes and tried concentrating on Damon, but it didn't help. All she could think about was how closely the color of Damon's hair matched Philip's.

It's only a mindless chemical reaction, she assured herself. Purely physical. The kind of thing that writers had been immortalizing in song and legend since time immemorial. And the very ferocity of her attraction guaranteed that it would quickly consume itself and burn out. A seed of doubt floated through her mind, but she refused to allow it to take root. She was a competent, modern woman who was more than capable of handling an unwanted sexual attraction, starting right now. She would look at him and see nothing but a superb physical specimen.

Ginny slowly raised her head and looked at Philip. Only a superb physical... Her determination wavered as he raised his hand and the muscles in his chest rippled. She found herself wondering what it would feel like if he were to hold her close to his chest. Close enough to feel the movement of those muscles. Close enough...

"No, I don't think the boy is Creon's."

Philip's curt words ripped through the sensual fog that had entrapped her, and her arms tightened protectively around Damon's defenseless little body. Grimly, Ginny bit back a furious retort. Yelling at him wouldn't help Beth. It would only make Philip feel justified in his pigheaded opinion. Besides, what Philip Lysander thought wasn't all that important in the final analysis, she reminded herself. It was what Jason Papas thought that counted.

"We'll be there tomorrow morning, Jason." Philip hung up the phone and turned to Ginny, frowning when he noticed how rigidly she was holding herself in the chair. She looked brittle enough to break, and there was a deep flush on her pale cheeks.

"Umm..." he began, not sure what he wanted to say.

"What?" Ginny clipped the word out, her eyes focused on a point beyond his left shoulder.

Was she embarrassed? he wondered. Embarrassed because he had so easily seen through her lies? Or angry that he had?

He watched as she leaned over the boy and the light from the lamp created golden sparkles in her hair. How could she look like a Botticelli Madonna and yet have had an affair with another woman's husband?

Philip watched the graceful movement of her hand and she swept back a tendril of hair that had escaped her chignon. What would it feel like to have her hair brush across his skin? He clenched his teeth as he felt himself reacting to the thought. The urge to touch her again was fast reaching a compulsion. A compulsion that worried him. He knew her to be a fraud, preying on a sick old man, so how could he be attracted to her?

"No one is ever going to believe that you're supposed to be my lover," he snapped, irritated at the way she refused to look at him. As if he were the one who was doing something wrong.

Ginny cautiously looked up and then wished she hadn't

when her eyes landed on the slight swell visible beneath his towel. Determinedly, she dragged her gaze upward to his face.

"Might I remind you that pretending we are lovers was your bright idea, not mine," she said. "No one who knows me would believe it."

"Why not?"

"Because the men I date are all calm, reasonable men who examine the facts before they leap to conclusions."

"They sound like bloodless bores!"

Ginny frowned at him, refusing to admit even to herself that some of them had been just the faintest bit stultifying.

"They are men of high principles." She retreated into platitudes.

"You're trying to tell me that your dates have all been men of high principles, and yet you claim that a married man is your son's father?" he asked scathingly.

"Be—" Ginny hastily caught herself and rushed on. "I didn't know he was married. He certainly never said so."

"He wore a wedding ring."

"Not in New York he didn't! And all that's immaterial." Ginny tried to redirect the conversation. She most emphatically didn't want to discuss her love life—such as it was— with Philip. She was edgy enough.

"It isn't immaterial that no one will believe that we are lovers."

"You could take out a newspaper ad!"

"Lovers should be comfortable around each other," he persisted.

Ginny grimaced. She didn't think she'd ever feel comfortable around him.

"We can start the process by you touching me." Philip walked over to where she was sitting, stopping scant inches from her.

She could smell the faint cedary fragrance of the soap he'd just used. It reminded her of Christmas and the anticipation that she always felt. As if something wondrous were about to happen. An anticipation much like that which gripped her now.

Touch him? Ginny considered his command. Where? Her eyes lingered on the contrast between his snowy white towel and the dark tone of his skin. Unconsciously, she rubbed the fingers of her free hand over her skirt to try to stop the tingling sensation that danced over them.

Touching him was definitely not a good idea, her mind decided even while her fingers curled in anticipation. But what could it hurt? Ginny tried to rationalize her growing need. In fact, it might help to speed up the time when her fascination with him would fade. And it wasn't as if she could do more than touch him. Not while she was cradling a sleeping baby.

Giving in to the temptation, Ginny reached out and poked his thigh with a fingertip. There was no give. He was solid muscle.

"Oh, for the..." Philip grabbed her hand and pressed it flat against his bare thigh.

Heat from his body flowed into her receptive flesh, loosening her inhibitions. Tentatively she moved her hand slightly, shivering as the hair on his leg scraped abrasively over her palm. To her mingled dismay and relief, Philip suddenly stepped back.

"It's a start," he muttered, and it seemed to Ginny that his voice was deeper.

Could he have been affected by her touch? Was that why he'd retreated? It was an intriguing thought, but not a relevant one, Ginny told herself. It didn't matter what Philip felt because she couldn't allow anything to develop between them. Beth was counting on her to get Jason Papas

to acknowledge Damon's right to the family's financial
support, and she couldn't do that if she were to become
emotionally involved with what appeared to be the main
opposition to the idea.

"There's a nursery at the end of the hall off the kitchen
that my sisters use when they stay at the apartment," Philip
said. "The boy can sleep there. Your luggage is in the
bedroom beside it."

Without another word, he turned and left the room. A
minute later she heard the sound of his bedroom door slam
shut.

"And a good-night to you, too," Ginny muttered as she
got to her feet, being careful not to jar the sleeping baby.
Things would be better after a good night's sleep, she told
herself as she went to find the nursery. At least she had the
comfort of knowing that they couldn't get much worse!

Absently, Philip pulled his towel off and dropped it on
the thick plush carpet. Her continued insistence that Creon
was the boy's father annoyed him, but didn't really surprise
him. Having come this far, she would hardly be likely to
change her story simply because he told her he knew that
she was lying. She was probably thinking that she would
have better luck at convincing a lonely old man that the
boy was his grandson.

Philip shoved his fingers through his damp hair in frustration. He knew she was lying. She had to be. Creon
couldn't have had an affair with another woman because
Lydia would have said something about it. She would have
asked his advice about what to do, and she hadn't. She'd
never said a word against Creon.

He paused as he suddenly realized something. Lydia had
never discussed Creon with him. She mentioned Jason occasionally, and she was always talking about her daughters,

but he couldn't ever remember her saying anything about Creon. A trickle of unease oozed through him. Was there some significance to her silence?

He didn't know, and there was no way he could ask her without revealing what he was trying to hide. And he couldn't risk that. Lydia had always been the most sensitive of his sisters. The most vulnerable. Creon's death had hit her very hard. She'd lost weight she couldn't afford to lose, and her always reserved personality had become almost withdrawn. If she were to find out that a beautiful woman had suddenly appeared, claiming to have had Creon's son, it could push her so deeply into her shell she might never be able to climb out. A feeling of desperation gripped him.

He had to protect Lydia. But could he? For the moment, Ginny Alton was willing to go along with the charade that the boy was his, but how long her cooperation would last was anyone's guess.

Philip dressed as he considered his limited options. He needed a lever to use against her, but what? Maybe the fact that Creon hadn't been seeing her while he'd been in New York? It wasn't much, but if he could find out how Creon had spent his time when he'd been in New York last year, perhaps it would convince Ginny that her claim wouldn't stand up to an investigation.

Philip picked up the phone and dialed the number of his company's New York office. His manager wouldn't be there at this time of night, but he could leave a message on Essing's voice mail telling him what he wanted him to do. With luck he'd have a report by tomorrow.

In the meantime, he'd simply have to keep as close to Ginny as he could to make sure she didn't do or say anything to upset Lydia. He'd stay very close. Philip felt a surge of anticipation that made him vaguely uneasy. Since he couldn't explain it, he ignored it and went to his study

to go over the latest developments in the labor problems at
one of his Athens' factories.

The following day dawned clear and sunny, unlike Ginny's mood. To her dismay, even though she was now well
rested, her first view of Philip over the breakfast table was
enough to convince her that a good night's sleep hadn't
changed anything. He still had a very unsettling effect on
her central nervous system. Even the fact that he was casually dressed in tan slacks and a powder blue knit shirt
didn't help.

Sitting down across from Philip, she gave Damon his
bottle. That meant that the only thing she could do was to
simply wait her compulsion out.

"Don't you ever feed the boy any real food?"

Ginny looked up to see Philip frowning at Damon's bottle.

"Damon. His name is Damon. And this is real food if
you happen to be four months old."

"He needs solid food," Philip insisted. "Some cereal
like this." He held up a spoonful of the oatmeal he was
eating.

Ginny fixed him with the gimlet stare she used on irrational clients who wanted to plunge into the stock market
with no plan of action. "He has already shown signs of
some nasty allergies, so if you even come near him with
that stuff, I'll..."

Philip looked at her ferocious expression and was hard-
pressed not to laugh. She looked like an angry lioness about
to defend her lone cub from mortal danger. A flicker of
tenderness unexpectedly curled through him. She really was
a good mother. It was too bad she hadn't been as careful
about who she went to bed with. Her lover couldn't have

been much of a man to have gotten her pregnant and then deserted her.

"You'll what?" he asked curiously, when she didn't finish her sentence.

"You'll see," Ginny promised darkly, having no idea what kind of threat might work on him. Probably none, she conceded. Philip Lysander appeared to be a man who was used to having his every whim catered to. Much as Creon had been.

To her surprise, his lips suddenly tightened. "If you repeat one word of your lies about Creon to Lydia, I'll make you rue the day you were born."

"And here I was afraid to descend to clichés," she scoffed.

"I mean it! As far as Lydia is concerned, the boy is mine." His voice was cold enough to freeze water.

What would it be like to have someone love you so much that they would be willing to go to such extremes to protect your peace of mind? Ginny wondered. The men she'd dated over the years had all treated her as the competent professional she was. They had respected her enough to allow her to solve her own problems. Which was what she wanted, she assured herself. She was strong enough to fight her own battles. She glanced down at Damon who was devouring his breakfast.

"I'll be in the study making a few phone calls," Philip said coldly as he got up from the table. "As soon as the boy is finished, we'll leave for Jason's."

Ginny watched until he disappeared into his study. "I wonder what his blood pressure is?" she murmured to Damon. "At least, he doesn't hold anything in."

Would he make love with the same intensity? It didn't matter how he made love. She throttled her curiosity. Philip Lysander's love life had nothing to do with her. Determinedly, Ginny focused her attention on Damon, trying to use her love for him to drive out her fascination with Philip. It was a dismal failure.

The trip from Athens to Glifadha took an hour and a half. An interminable hour and a half. Between her agitation at being cooped up in a closed car with Philip, her nervousness over the upcoming interview with Jason Papas and the fact that Damon cried for most of the trip, Ginny was a bundle of nerves by the time Philip pulled up in front of Jason's rambling white villa.

Ginny quickly climbed out of the car, unbuckled Damon from his car seat and cradled his hot, sweaty little body against her shoulder.

"Come on." Philip grabbed her arm and hurried her inside.

Ginny quietly followed him through the huge house because she wasn't sure that he'd let go of her, and she didn't want to get into an undignified scuffle with Philip under Jason Papas's nose.

Philip finally stopped in the open doorway of a large study.

"Is that the child?"

Ginny looked in the direction of the harsh voice to find a gaunt old man, who had to be Jason Papas, standing by the window eyeing her with distaste. Unconsciously, her chin lifted, and she stared back at him with equal distaste. If Jason hadn't raised Creon to believe that he had a right to take what he wanted from whomever he wanted it, then poor Beth would never have been put in this situation.

"Yes," Philip answered when Ginny remained silent.

"Bring him here," Jason ordered Ginny.

Ginny walked to within a few feet of Jason and shifted Damon slightly so that his face was no longer hidden against her neck. She watched as Jason inched closer to the child as if drawn against his will. It was impossible for her to tell what the old man thought because other than the glitter in his eyes, which could have been anything from anger to happiness, his features were blank.

Unfortunately, Damon was not so reticent about expressing an opinion. He took one look at his grandfather and let out a howl.

Using Damon's reaction as an excuse, Ginny retreated. "Damon doesn't like strangers," she said coolly.

"And you claim he's my grandson?" Jason sneered.

"I don't claim it. I know it."

"You're pretty enough to tempt a man to forget his marriage vows," Jason said, and Ginny didn't make the mistake of reading a compliment into his words. "But my son would never sully his honor with the likes of you. The truth is—"

"You wouldn't know the truth if it hit you over the head!" Ginny decided that it was time to firmly establish a few ground rules. Such as the fact that she would not allow herself to be verbally abused. "You can blather on about Creon's so-called honor till the day you die, but it won't change the facts one iota. And I'll give you another news flash. I did not fly halfway across the world to serve as a verbal punching bag for your prejudices."

Jason glared at her. "So what are you going to do? Leave? If you do, you'll never see a drachma of my money."

"That will be for the courts to decide," Ginny retorted. She didn't know if Beth would take her quest for recognition of Damon that far, but it wouldn't hurt Jason to believe it.

"The courts!" A deep flush burned high on his thin cheekbones. "You actually dare to threaten me?"

"No," Ginny said flatly. "I'm not threatening anything.

I'm telling you. Damon is entitled to his father's support, and if it takes a lawsuit to obtain it..." She allowed her voice to trail away.

"Why, you immoral slut!" Jason's lips compressed as if he'd just bitten down on something very bitter.

"That's enough! Both of you." To Ginny's surprise, Philip intervened. "This is getting us nowhere, Jason. I'll show Ginny the nursery, and we can discuss this later."

The only thing Ginny wanted to discuss at that precise moment was the quickest way to return to New York. But the memory of Beth's desperate face stilled the words in her throat. Beth was counting on her.

Ginny tensed as Philip took her arm and hustled her away from Jason. And there was another reason why she wasn't quite ready to leave, she admitted honestly. If she were to leave Greece now, she would probably never see Philip Lysander again, and if she didn't see him again she couldn't find out why he exerted such an unprecedented pull on her emotions. Somehow she needed to find out the reason for her attraction. She needed a rational explanation so that she could go back to being comfortable with herself.

"Jason isn't normally so..." Philip gestured impotently.

"You mean no one normally gives the old tyrant any opposition!" Ginny said dryly. "Having met the father, I suddenly understand why Creon was such a self-centered, self-absorbed twit."

Philip glanced at her. "If you felt that way, why did you have an affair with him?"

Ginny bit her tongue in annoyance at her hasty words. The more she became involved with the Papas family, the harder it was for her to remember that she was the one who had supposedly loved Creon.

"He could be very charming when things were going his way," she finally said. "It's only when his duplicity caught up with him in the form of Damon that he showed his true colors."

Philip frowned as he suddenly remembered something his mother had said a few years ago about the way Jason indulged Creon's every wish.

"Philip." A soft, hesitant voice called to them from a small sitting room as they passed the open archway.

Ginny stopped, forcing Philip to, also. A petite, dark-haired woman somewhere in her thirties was standing across the room. She started toward them, a warm smile on her face. A shard of some dark emotion ripped through Ginny as Philip's lips curved in a loving smile. A smile that was reflected in his dark eyes.

He enveloped the woman in a bear hug and swung her around in a circle. Setting her down on her feet and keeping a protective arm around her shoulders, he turned her toward Ginny. "Lydia, this is Ginny Alton and her son, Damon. Ginny, this is my sister Lydia."

Philip's dark eyes held an unspoken warning as he stared at Ginny.

"Hello," Ginny said, telling herself that the relief she felt at discovering this was his sister was only because the situation didn't need the complication of a jealous girlfriend of Philip's in the house.

"Good morning." Lydia gave Ginny an uncertain smile as if not sure how to greet her.

Which made two of them who weren't comfortable with the situation, Ginny thought wryly.

Lydia's smile widened, becoming more natural, as Damon gave a gurgle and waved a fist at her. "What a darling little boy. You must be very proud of him. My husband always wanted a boy, but I never..." Lydia sighed. "He was so disappointed when our last daughter was born."

Ginny stared at Lydia in horrified disbelief. Daughter!

Last daughter! Creon not only had a wife tucked away in
Greece while he was seducing Beth, but he had children!

"Umm, Ginny..." Philip began, not liking the glint in
Ginny's eye.

Ginny ignored him. "How many daughters do you have,
Lydia?"

"Three," Lydia said. "Maria is three, Ianthe is two, and
little Jasmine is just five months old."

One month older than Damon! Impotent fury poured
through Ginny. If she could have somehow gotten her
hands on Creon, she would have cheerfully throttled him.

"Damon looks very Greek," Lydia observed with a side-
ways glance at Philip.

Philip winced at the accusation he could see in Lydia's
eyes. He didn't want his sister to think that he was the kind
of heedless, selfish man who would get a woman pregnant
and allow his child to be born a bastard. But the alternative
was to tell her what Ginny was claiming, and that was
unthinkable.

Telling himself that once he had pried the real name of
Damon's father out of Ginny he would tell Lydia the truth,
he took a deep breath and forced out the lie. "I think he
looks a lot like me."

As if on cue, Damon emitted an angry howl.

Ginny gave Philip a limpid smile. "He certainly acts like
you."

"Poor little thing," Lydia sympathized. "He sounds
very unhappy."

"He needs to be changed, some food and a nap—in that
order," Ginny said.

"If you'd feed him something with a little bulk to it, he
wouldn't always be hungry," Philip muttered.

Lydia ignored him. "I will take you to the nursery. It
should have everything you need."

Ginny followed Lydia, feeling as if she'd done nothing but trail along behind people since she'd arrived in Greece. Unable to resist the impulse, she glanced over her shoulder at Philip. He hadn't moved. He was still standing there, although with the window at his back, she couldn't tell if he were watching them or not. He was simply a large, dark form looming in the middle of the room.

Like Nemesis. Her own personal Nemesis. Ginny resisted the childish impulse to stick out her tongue at him.

Lydia glanced from Ginny back to Philip and said, "You must love him very much."

"My feelings for your brother are very strong," Ginny said with absolute sincerity.

Lydia patted Ginny's arm comfortingly. "Do not worry. He will do his duty by you. I will call the family."

"The family?" Ginny said weakly, not liking the sound of that. This scenario needed less players, not more.

Lydia nodded emphatically. "Mama and my sisters. They will talk to Philip."

He had mentioned sisters when he'd explained the nursery in his apartment, Ginny remembered. At the time she'd been too tired to wonder about it. "How many sisters do you have?"

"Five. We are all older than Philip."

"I can imagine that he would have been enough to deter your parents from trying again."

Lydia looked at Ginny uncertainly as if not sure how she was supposed to respond. Finally, she gave an unsteady gurgle of laughter—as if laughing weren't something she did very often. As it probably wasn't, Ginny thought. Having been married to a man like Creon would have squelched even a confirmed optimist's sense of humor.

"Please don't call the family, Lydia."

"But Philip must do his duty toward you," Lydia protested.

"I most emphatically don't want a man to 'do his duty toward me.'" Ginny wrinkled her nose in distaste at the idea.

Lydia sighed. "Yes, duty is cold comfort. But if you do not want to marry Philip then why did you come to Greece?"

Ginny felt like screaming in frustration. How could such a simple thing like going to see Damon's grandfather have evolved into such a complicated tangle of lies?

For once, Ginny was relieved when Damon started to cry, because Lydia seemed to forget her question.

"Come. The nursery is this way. I will introduce you to Nanny who looks after Jasmine. Miss Welbourne is the older girls' governess, but she and they are spending a few weeks in Paris with my mother."

Ginny felt anger bubble through her. Lydia had a nanny and a governess and, undoubtedly, a staff of servants to run this palatial villa, while poor Beth had had to move in with Ginny because she couldn't afford to keep her own apartment while she wasn't teaching. Ginny glanced over at Lydia's sad face and her anger deepened, becoming all the stronger because she didn't have anyone to vent it on. None of this mess was Lydia's fault. In a way, she was as much Creon's victim as Beth was.

No, Ginny hastily banished the thought. She couldn't begin to worry about Lydia.

The nursery was located in the very back of the house and was luxurious to the point of opulence. Ginny shivered as she looked around. She found so much luxury almost oppressive. Nanny, however, was another matter. She was a cheerful, plump little Englishwoman of indeterminate middle age who reminded Ginny of a wren.

While Nanny went to heat a bottle of formula for Damon, Lydia urged Ginny closer to the crib in the corner. It was elaborately hung with what looked like antique Mechlin lace and contained a sleeping baby.

"This is Jasmine," Lydia announced. "She is such a good little thing."

"She's very pretty," Ginny muttered, trying to absorb the fact that this child was Damon's half sister.

"Yes, she is," Lydia said with such pride that it unexpectedly made Ginny want to cry. She just wasn't sure who she wanted to cry for. Lydia, the two babies, Beth or for herself who was standing squarely in the middle of it all.

"I will leave you in Nanny's capable hands while I see about lunch," Lydia said.

Ginny watched her go with a feeling of regret. Lydia's was the first friendly face she had seen since she'd arrived.

"Here you are." Nanny bustled back with a warm bottle for Damon.

"Thank you." Sitting down in a large well-cushioned rocker, Ginny gave Damon his bottle. As he gulped his formula, she slowly rocked back and forth, allowing her mind to wander. To her dismay, it immediately wandered to Philip and how he'd looked last night wrapped in that scrap of a white towel and nothing else. She swallowed uneasily and tried to banish the image, but it kept leaking out of her memory. She finally decided that there wasn't anything wrong with daydreaming about Philip. It wasn't as if she were some naive, impressionable fool who couldn't tell erotic fantasies from reality.

A feeling of heaviness descended over her like the soft enveloping weight of a down-filled comforter as Ginny imagined herself grabbing the end of Philip's towel and tugging. Of pulling it loose. Ginny ran her tongue over her suddenly dry lips as she pictured him nude. It was an image powerful enough to send a flush over her entire body, and she wiggled slightly in the rocker.

It was Damon's muttered protest that brought her up for air. "Sorry, sweet'n." She dropped a kiss on Damon' small head. "I got carried away." Her mind obligingly fitted an image of Philip carrying her to a soft bed.... She had to stop this, she told herself. Daydreaming was one thing. Even erotic fantasies were acceptable. But not compulsive fixations. She would think of something else. Determinedly she focused on what looked to be a real Degas painting on the wall opposite her and forced herself to mentally review the facts of the Argentine company she was evaluating for her firm. It was a struggle but she was finally able to concentrate on emerging markets.

Half an hour later, Damon was sleeping peacefully under Nanny's watchful eye, and Ginny left the nursery, hoping for a few minutes of quiet away from any emotional distractions.

It wasn't until she reached the sitting room where she'd met Lydia that she realized that she didn't have anyplace to go. No one had told her where her room was, and she could hardly wander about a strange house, opening doors looking to see where her luggage had been put.

Crossing the empty room, Ginny stepped outside through the open French doors onto the flagstone paved terrace. The breeze off the sea was laden with salt and carried a faint tang of adventure that drew her toward the white, sandy beach.

She needed to think about what had happened since she'd arrived in Greece. She needed to try to decide what to do next. To weigh what effect finding out that Beth's Creon had not only had a wife, but three small children would have on her cousin's peace of mind. Ginny winced at the thought of telling her. But if she didn't tell Beth, and Beth found out from someone else....

Glancing back over her shoulder, Ginny stared at the gleaming villa and shuddered. Someone like Jason Papas would tell poor Beth in as brutal a way as possible. In a way, Ginny couldn't be sorry that Creon hadn't been able to marry Beth. Beth would never have thrived in the atmosphere here at the villa. She would have been suffocated. Much as she suspected Lydia had been.

Forget Lydia, Ginny told herself. Concentrate on regaining your emotional equilibrium so that you can tackle Philip again. An unconscious smile curved her mouth as she imagined throwing herself at Philip and wrestling him to the ground. A sudden feeling of lightheartedness swept over her, and she kicked off her sandals and began to walk through the surf, letting the waves wash over her bare feet.

Three

"The boy looks like Creon." The words seemed torn from Jason.

"He looks like a baby with a dark complexion and dark hair," Philip insisted. "That hardly makes him Creon's."

Jason grimaced and took another swallow of the whiskey he'd poured himself.

"I left a message last night with my office manager in New York to look into Creon's activities while he was there last year. No doubt he'll be able to tell us that Creon spent all of his time at his apartment or at work."

"I don't trust her!" Jason burst out. "She's too pretty. Too…" Jason struggled to find words. "Too unbending. She looked at me as if I were…" A dark red flush of anger scorched his face.

Unbending? Philip weighed Jason's description. Possibly, he conceded. Certainly Ginny Alton would not be easily swayed, but he found the quality intriguing, unlike Jason who expected a woman to agree with his every pronouncement. Much as Lydia had done with Creon, Philip suddenly realized.

"Creon wouldn't have done it," Jason insisted.

Me thinks thou doth protest too much. A line from some Shakespearean play he'd been forced to read in school drifted through Philip's mind. Hastily he banished the thought. This was no time for him to begin second-guessing himself. Lydia was depending on him. He had to expose Ginny's lies for what they were.

"I don't know what the world is coming to," Jason muttered. "In my day, that sort of woman would have known her place."

Ginny's place? Philip let Jason's tirade roll over him. Where was Ginny Alton's place? In his bed? A heavy weight seemed to settle on his chest, constricting his breathing as he imagined her sprawled in the middle of his bed.

She'd be wearing silk, he decided. Silk to complement her satiny skin. Thin, green silk. The color of new growth in the springtime. And lace. He took a deep breath, savoring the provocative thought. Lace to almost cover her breasts. And through the lace, her pale pink flesh would gleam like a perfect pearl.

"She's nothing but a common slut," Jason complained.

"Ginny Alton is certainly not common and we don't know that she is a slut," Philip instinctively defended her.

"Don't tell me that you want to take another man's leavings?" Jason sneered.

"I wonder what would happen to men if women were to adopt that restrictive a policy," Philip said impatiently.

"Women expect men to have experience." Jason justified his double standard. "Only a whore goes to bed with

a man outside of marriage. You think you have all th
answers, boy, but your father would have agreed with me.

Philip opened his mouth to tell Jason a few other releva
things that his father had believed in when a flash of brigl
blue-green caught his eye. He hurried over to the study'
French doors and looked outside. Ginny was hurrying dow
the beach away from the villa.

The breeze off the sea was blowing her golden ha
around her bare shoulders. She shouldn't be out there in
sundress without a hat, Philip thought. She wasn't used t
the hot Greek sun and with her fair coloring she could bur
badly in a very short time.

"What are you looking at?" Jason demanded.

Suddenly heartily sick of the old man's carping, Phili
felt an overpowering urge to escape. To escape into th
brilliant sunlight outside. Besides, it was his duty to war
Ginny of the dangers of the Greek sun, he rationalized hi
urge to go after her.

"The sea." Philip gave Jason part of the truth. "I thin
I'll go for a walk on the beach."

"I don't know where you get your energy." Jaso
sagged into his chair and closed his eyes. "I'm going t
take a nap."

Philip hurried out onto the terrace. Kicking off his shoe
and socks, he rolled up his pant legs and hurried after he

Ginny stopped as she heard the distant sound of a moto
and shielding her eyes, stared out across the water. Ther
was a speedboat zipping along and filled with laughing peo
ple who looked as if they were having the time of thei
lives.

She sighed, wishing that she could capture some of thei
exuberance. It might help to dilute Jason's hostility.

A larger than normal wave washed over her bare leg

and splashed the hem of her skirt. It felt refreshingly cool in relation to the burning sun, and Ginny dug her toes into the sand, relishing the gritty sensation. Greece was such a gorgeous place. Someday, when this whole mess was simply a bad memory, she'd have to return and enjoy the sun and the sand and the sea.

A sudden prickle of awareness tightened her skin. As f... Turning, she saw Philip jogging toward her, and a flare of excitement tore through her. He looked different with his pant legs rolled up almost to his knees and his bare feet sending up splashes of water as he bounded through the surf. Younger, almost carefree.

Even so, no one would ever take Philip Lysander for a beachcomber. There was too much barely leashed energy swirling around him and it kept leaking out to infect the people in his vicinity. Like her, she thought ruefully.

What would it take to relax him? The aftermath of making love? Would that be enough? Ginny ran her tongue over her wind-dried lips as an image of his tanned body lying angled in bed sheets hit her with the force of a blow. What would he be like after having made love to a woman? Would he be tender? Would he hold his partner and share the moment with her?

"Wait for me!" Philip's shouted order broke into her daydreams, and she grimaced. He probably wouldn't be one whit different than at any other time.

Ginny waited until he reached her and then launched an offensive. "Why? Have you come to tell me that Jason has suddenly remembered his manners?"

"I know Jason can be a little difficult." Philip ignored her snort of derision. "But he's defending his son's honor and—"

"I very much doubt that. He's simply reacting from the monumental depths of his own prejudices."

"He is a little set in his ways, but memories of his so
are all he has left. Why can't you see that?" Philip's voic
hardened in frustration.

"Because I'm too busy seeing Damon's side of things.'

"His interests would be better served if you'd ask hi
real father to support him!"

"Why, you sanctimonious..." Ginny sputtered. Infuri
ated, she spun on her heel to leave him to his blind stupid
ity.

"Don't turn your back on me!" Philip grabbed her by
the arm. "I haven't finished talking to you."

"Too bad! I'm more than finished with you. And tak
your hands off me."

"Or what?" he mocked her. "You'll make me?"

Ginny looked at his smug expression and felt a cold fury
shoot through her. She wanted to wipe his smirk away and
never mind the consequences.

Impulsively acting on the desire, she hooked her foo
around his ankle and pushed against his chest with he
palms. The maneuver didn't quite work the way the self
defense instructor at the Y had said it would. Philip los
his balance and fell all right, but since he hadn't let go o
her arm, she fell on top of him.

The impact drove the air from her lungs and for an ag
onizing moment Ginny fought to force air back into them
And then, once she could breathe, she became excruciat
ingly aware of his hard-muscled body pushing into her
much softer one. The delectable sensation fanned the com
plex mix of emotions already swirling through her. Ginny
stared at the firm line of Philip's lips and trembled. She
wanted to feel them against her own. She wanted to taste
them. To nibble and bite on them. To learn their every
nuance.

Her breathing shortened, and the fierce sun beating dow

on her seemed to be melting her body, making it flow into him.

Ginny tensed as she felt Philip's fingers spear through her hair to cup the back of her head. She should move, the faint voice of sanity urged. She should roll off him, scramble to her feet and run as if all the devils in hell were on her heels. But the warning seemed to be coming from a great distance. From a cold, abstract place that had no relevance to the pulsating world of the senses that held her captive.

Her gaze moved upward from his tantalizing lips and was immediately captured by the hot glow burning deep in his dark eyes. Whatever Philip thought about her as a person, he appeared to be as susceptible to her physically as she was to him. The knowledge added a sense of power to her already hopelessly muddled emotions.

A wave broke against her legs, and the warm, caressing water seemed to dissolve the last of her inhibitions. She was incapable of resisting when Philip tugged her head down. His lips brushed against hers in a feather-light kiss that sent tremors rippling through her. Mindlessly, she pressed harder, wanting to intensify the illusive sensation trickling through her.

As if he understood her need, Philip traced over the line of her closed lips with his hot, seeking tongue.

A tiny moan of pleasure bubbled out of her throat, and she opened her mouth to him. The rough warmth of his tongue scraped over her inner cheek and sent a tingling sensation over her nerves. Blindly reacting to her need to touch him, Ginny ran her fingers through his hair, gripping his warm scalp as she sought an anchor in the storm of sensation he was arousing.

Shifting slightly, Philip rolled onto his side, still keeping Ginny pressed tightly against him.

His lips left her mouth to wander over her face, dropping insubstantial kisses as he moved. Ginny found it more frustrating than satisfying. Like nibbling on carrot sticks while everyone else was indulging in hot fudge sundaes. She wanted him to kiss her properly. With force and passion. She wanted...

His hand suddenly pushed aside the thin strap of her sundress to expose one of her breasts, and Ginny shivered. Her thoughts blurred, becoming a confusing clamor of need as Philip rubbed his palm back and forth over the slope of her satiny skin.

"You're so soft," Philip whispered, and Ginny could feel his breath against her skin, tightening her excitement to unbearable levels. "So touchable." His tongue darted out, and he licked her taut nipple.

A shard of desire shot through Ginny, making her jerk convulsively. The intensity of her reaction frightened her badly. Badly enough to allow her to break free of the sensual spell that had captured her. Jerking away from him, she scrambled to her knees and awkwardly fumbled to straighten her bodice with fingers made clumsy from thwarted desire.

Hurriedly she glanced around but the beach was still deserted. Not that she had cared, she admitted with a growing sense of unreality. When Philip had kissed her, she hadn't cared who might be watching. All that she cared about was that he not stop.

Ginny gulped. That wasn't like her, she thought in confusion. Not at all. Never before had she been so involved in a kiss that she had forgotten everything under its impact. Always before some part of her mind had remained aloof, an onlooker to what was happening.

"This won't do," she muttered aloud.

"Damn right it won't." Philip stood up and began to brush the sand off his wet pants.

Ginny peered up at his large body looming above her, her eyes drawn like a magnet to the obvious evidence of his arousal. He looked so large. So quintessentially masculine. Like one of the Greek gods come down from Mount Olympus to dally with a mortal woman.

"I'm far too old to settle for snatched kisses on the beach. I want to go to bed with you." Philip voiced the desire that had been building in him from the first moment he'd seen her. There was no reason why he shouldn't, he rationalized. The fact that she was trying to pass her child off as Creon's was really irrelevant since he knew it to be a lie.

A wave of longing to do what Philip suggested swept through Ginny, but she determinedly beat it back. It was a very bad idea. One of the very worst ones she'd ever had. She knew it. So why didn't her body know it, too? The disquieting question popped into her mind. Why did her body want to jump into bed with Philip and damn the consequences?

"Oh, hell!" Ginny muttered in frustrated confusion as she lurched to her feet. She was a modern woman in command of her passions, not a slave to them, she reminded herself. Simply because she wanted—*craved* to make love to Philip, didn't mean that she had to give in to it.

"I do not have the slightest desire to make love to you." She put every ounce of emphasis she could into the words.

Philip lightly flicked his finger over the taut bud of her nipple clearly outlined beneath her wet sundress. "No?"

"I won't make love to you," she rephrased.

"Why not?" His voice lowered seductively, and Ginny felt a quiver of response tremble through her. It scared her. Instinctively she took a step backward. She wasn't sure how long she could hold out against both him and her own desires if he were to take her in his arms again.

Turning on her heel, she hurried back to the villa, praying that Philip wouldn't follow her. She desperately needed some time alone to regain her equilibrium. Say two or three years.

Philip watched her go, his attention focused on the way her wet skirt clung to her legs. He wanted to feel those legs wrapped around him as he drove deep into her willing body. Annoyed, he kicked at the sand. Ginny wanted it, too. He'd felt the depth of her response. So why wouldn't she go to bed with him? It wasn't as if she were some wide-eyed virgin ignorant of the pleasures to be found in sex.

Thoughtfully, Philip began to walk farther on down the beach as he considered the situation. Ginny might not be an innocent, but there were times when she certainly acted like one. Suddenly feeling lighthearted, he started to jog. Somehow he'd get her into his bed. All it would take was a little planning coupled with patience.

Except for one quick glance over her shoulder, Ginny was careful not to look after Philip as she made her way back to the villa. She felt like something the sea had washed up. She wiggled her shoulders as the grains of sand trapped in her bodice irritated her tender skin. What she needed was a hot shower and dry clothes. And not to run across Jason Papas.

Fortunately, the only person on the terrace was a maid who showed Ginny to the room she'd been given. Ginny quickly showered, and after checking to make sure that Damon was still napping, returned to the terrace where she found Lydia sitting in a lounger under a grape arbor, knitting a small, red sweater. Deciding this might be a good time to try to find out more about the situation, Ginny joined her.

Lydia looked up from her knitting and smiled warmly at Ginny. "I like your sundress. It reminds me of a strawberry ice-cream cone."

"Thank you. Do you live here with Mr. Papas all the time?" Ginny asked, trying to make the question sound casual.

Lydia gave her a resigned smile. "Creon preferred that we live with his father because he had to travel so much. That way he could be sure that I was not alone."

And also be sure that you were safely tucked away somewhere where you couldn't discover what he was up to, Ginny added cynically.

"And I am company for Jason, too, since his wife died many years ago," Lydia added.

"What about company for you?" Ginny asked, curious about how Lydia's mind operated.

Lydia blinked. "Me? Why would I need company? I have my children."

"But what about friends your own age?" Ginny said, appalled at the picture of isolation Lydia was presenting.

Lydia smiled sadly. "Once I would have agreed with you, but now…" She shrugged. "Now I am a widow."

"A very attractive, very young widow," Ginny said.

Lydia glanced around as if to make sure no one could hear her, and then whispered, "But I lack sex appeal."

The suppressed pain in Lydia's voice made Ginny wonder if perhaps Lydia knew more about Creon's affairs than Philip thought.

"All women have sex appeal, but not for all men." Ginny tried to comfort her. "Sex appeal, like beauty, tends to be in the eye of the beholder."

Lydia looked confused.

"I'll give you an example," Ginny elaborated. "You thought your husband was sexy, but—"

"No, I did not."

Ginny blinked, taken aback. "Then why on earth did you marry him?"

"Because I had to marry someone, and Creon was suitable."

"Suitable?" Ginny repeated blankly.

Lydia nodded. "Everyone said so. Mama, and my sisters and Philip and Jason and Creon. And Steward wasn't."

Ginny had the weird feeling that she'd stepped off what she thought was a stair and tumbled into an abyss.

"Who is Steward?" Ginny grabbed a promising conversational thread and pursued it.

Lydia sighed, and the sound was pregnant with suppressed longing. "Steward Morris is an English artist living here in Greece. He is very talented. Someday, everyone will be proud to say they knew him."

For *everyone*, read Philip and her family, Ginny translated.

"But he has no money."

"You have money," Ginny pointed out.

"Well, yes, but...the husband should have it."

"Nonsense! I agree that it makes life a lot easier if one of the partners has enough money to pay the bills, but for both of you to have it is overkill."

Lydia looked intrigued at the idea. "Do you really think so?"

"Yes, I do!" Ginny said emphatically. In some ways Lydia was as naive as poor Beth was. In fact, Lydia appeared to be a lot like Beth: shy, introverted and not very secure in her own charms. Apparently, Creon preferred emotionally immature women.

"Oh, I almost forgot, Ginny. We are having guests this evening. Mr. and Mrs. Stavrinidis and their daughter. I suggested to Jason that it might be better if he were to put them off for a few days, but he says that he needs to discuss business with Mr. Stavrinidis."

"Lovely, and what will the women talk about?" Ginny asked.

"You," Lydia said bluntly. "The Stavrinidises have a daughter that they had hoped..."

To marry off to Philip, Ginny finished the sentence, trying to ignore the sharp spurt of emotion she felt at the thought. Annoyance, she labeled the feeling. Annoyance at having to deal with yet one more complication.

"I am sorry." Lydia's soft voice recalled her. "I did not mean to worry you, but I feared that if you did not know about the Stavrinidises' daughter..."

"I'd be a sitting duck for all their little innuendos?" Ginny asked dryly.

Lydia giggled. "Anyone less like a duck I have yet to see. When the Stavrinidises see you, they will have no trouble understanding why Philip chose you."

"Philip hasn't chosen me."

"One has only to see the way he looks at you to know that what he feels is very strong. Once he becomes accustomed to the idea of marriage, he will be happy," Lydia insisted.

Ginny gave up. Without telling her the truth, there was no way she could convince Lydia that Philip wasn't about to marry her, and she didn't want to do that. Not only would it make Philip furious, but she wasn't sure if she'd be doing Lydia a kindness or not by telling her that her dead husband had been an adulterous bastard.

Ginny tensed as she looked up and caught sight of Philip running toward the villa from the beach. She didn't want to see him now. Not until she had somehow managed to expunge from her mind the memory of her reaction to his kiss.

"I think I'll go check on Damon." Ginny hurriedly got to her feet.

"Why not wait for Philip and take him with you?" Lydia had also seen him.

"I've had more than enough of your precious brother for the moment," Ginny muttered.

To her surprise, Lydia giggled enchantingly. "I am going to enjoy having you for a sister, Ginny. You are as beautiful as the other women he usually dates, but you have more spirit. I think you will be good for him."

The other women? Lydia's words echoed in Ginny's head as she hurried to the nursery. How many "other women" did Philip have? Was he as much of a playboy as Creon had been? The idea bothered her on some level, and the fact that it did bothered her even more.

It wasn't any of her business if Philip Lysander was the premier playboy of the western world. Once she managed to settle Damon's future, she'd leave Greece and never see any of them again. And good riddance, she told herself, trying hard to believe it.

"Philip!" Jason stuck his head out the study doors and yelled as Philip approached the terrace. "Essings from your New York office is on the phone. He wants to talk to you."

Philip sprinted across the terrace and into the study. Taking the phone that Jason shoved at him, Philip switched it to speaker mode so that Jason could hear and said, "This is Lysander. What were you able to find out, Essings?"

"Good morning, sir. I talked to the doorman at the building where Mr. Papas had sublet an apartment, and he said that Mr. Papas always seemed to be in the company of a pretty blond woman.''

Philip frowned. Pretty? The doorman must be blind. Ginny was beautiful by anybody's standards.

''And I talked to the receptionist at the Papas offices and she said that Mr. Papas gave her instructions that when a Miss Alton called, she was to put her right through to him,'' Essings continued.

Philip glared at an innocent-looking painting of water lilies on the wall in front of him, wanting to smash something. So Ginny hadn't been lying. She had had an affair with Creon. How the hell could Creon have done that to Lydia? Lydia was kind and gentle and... And she didn't have one tenth of the sex appeal Ginny had.

His fingers clenched into fists in impotent frustration. Even he wasn't immune to Ginny's allure, and he was far more experienced than Creon had been.

''Um, Mr. Lysander, are you still there? Did you want me to keep looking into this?'' Essings's hesitant voice interrupted Philip's thoughts.

''No.'' Philip kept his inner turmoil out of his voice with an effort. ''That was all I wanted to know. I appreciate your efforts. Thank you.''

''You're welcome, Mr. Lysander. Glad to be of service.''

''Goodbye.'' Philip cut the connection.

''I don't believe it!'' Jason muttered. ''Creon would never have—''

''Creon did.'' Philip cut through Jason's denials. Philip walked over to the liquor cabinet and poured himself some whiskey. He took a hefty swallow, trying to drown the fury burning through him. It didn't help.

He shoved his long fingers through his hair. He could understand why Creon would have had an affair with Ginny. What was harder to understand was why Ginny had done it. As beautiful as she was, she could easily have found a man of her own. Why settle for another woman's? Could she have been telling the truth when she'd said that she hadn't known Creon was married?

"Just because they had an affair doesn't mean that Creon was the boy's father." Philip grasped at straws. If the boy wasn't Creon's, then Lydia wouldn't ever have to know. But if he was... A chill feathered down his spine at the thought of the inevitable repercussions if the boy really was Jason's grandson.

"That's true!" Jason eagerly agreed. "Why, a woman like that was probably sleeping with three or four men at the time."

"I've seen no evidence that Ginny Alton is promiscuous," Philip said sharply, remembering her hasty withdrawal on the beach when he'd touched her breasts. Her behavior simply didn't add up, he thought in frustration. He was missing something vital. But what?

"You're saying you think the boy is Creon's?" Jason demanded.

Philip rubbed the back of his neck. "I don't know. I hope not. For Lydia's sake." He took another gulp of whiskey. "But with what Essings found out, it's a distinct possibility."

"I won't take the word of a slut—"

"Her name is Ginny!" Philip's voice sliced across Jason's invective. "And unless you want me to start referring to Creon by a similarly uncomplimentary term, I suggest you remember it."

Jason eyed him in disbelief. "You are defending that..."

"I'm defending my sister from your son's philandering. And as I see it, the best way to do it is to find out the truth."

"And how do you propose we do that?" Jason snapped. "Creon is the only one who can tell us, and he's dead."

"I suggest we take a blood sample from you and the boy and have a geneticist compare them. If the boy really is your grandson, there should be some genetic points in common."

Jason pursed his thin lips as he considered the idea. "The woman will never allow it," he finally said. "It would expose her for the liar she is."

"I hadn't intended to ask her. She claims she wants the boy acknowledged. This will prove it one way or another. I see no reason to bother her with the details."

"All right," Jason said heavily. "I owe it to Creon's good name to prove that the boy isn't his. You arrange it."

"I'll have a nurse drive down from Athens to take the blood samples as soon as possible." Philip started to leave.

"Philip," Jason called after him.

Philip reluctantly paused in the doorway and looked back at Jason. He wanted to get away from the old man. The more he talked to him the less he liked him, even though he knew it wasn't really Jason's fault. He was only trying to protect his memories of his son, the same way he was trying to protect Lydia's peace of mind.

"I forgot to mention that the Stavrinidises will be joining us for dinner."

"Oh, hell!" Philip muttered to himself as he left. That was all he needed to make the day complete. Stavrinidis trying to involve him in some improbable business deal while his wife alternated between inane gossip and extolling the virtues of her daughter to him.

Philip stalked down the hallway toward his room, his steps slowing as he suddenly remembered something. Ginny had agreed to pretend to be his lover, and as his lover, in company at least, he would be able to indulge his desire to touch her. But should he? The knowledge that she really had been Creon's lover burned like acid at the edges of his desire.

Ginny had gone to bed with his brother-in-law. His defenseless sister's husband. Ginny had allowed Creon to kiss her and touch her and... Philip clenched his teeth against the provocative images that flooded his mind. They made him feel furious and totally impotent to do anything about it.

Because of Lydia, he told himself. Because he didn't want Lydia to be hurt anymore. But it was precisely because he didn't want Lydia hurt again that he had to continue with the fiction that Ginny was his lover and the boy was his son. In fact, he should probably elaborate on his charade to allay any lingering doubts Lydia might have. A tiny feeling of anticipation surfaced through the chaotic emotions swirling through him.

Closing his bedroom door behind him, he began to absently strip off his clothes as he considered exactly how far he should take his role of besotted lover at dinner.

As dinnertime approached, Ginny was beginning to wish she'd had the foresight to claim a headache and hide in her room. She wasn't sure she could get through a whole evening in Jason Papas's company without breaking down and screaming at him like a demented fishwife. Her brief attempt to settle matters with him earlier in the afternoon had convinced her that he was, without a doubt, the most obnoxious man she'd ever had the misfortune to meet.

And adding to her sense of ill-usage was the fact that Philip had disappeared somewhere without a word to her. She couldn't even ask Lydia where he'd gone because Lydia had spent the afternoon at the local church.

So Ginny had retreated to the nursery with Damon and,

while she dearly loved him, he was not the most stimulating of company.

"Ginny?" Lydia's soft voice sounded through Ginny's bedroom door.

"Come in," Ginny called.

Lydia pushed open the door and stepped inside. "I just came to see if..." Her voice trailed away.

Ginny looked down at her severely cut, black silk dress with its deeply scooped neckline and pencil-slim skirt, and then back at Lydia.

"Isn't my dress appropriate?" Ginny asked as she took in the high-collared, full-skirted dress Lydia was wearing. It reminded Ginny of something her mother might wear.

Lydia sighed. "You look fantastic, but then Philip's women always do."

"You make him sound like a sultan who keeps a harem." Ginny tried not to let Lydia's continued references to Philip's women bother her.

Lydia frowned thoughtfully. "No, it is not that. Actually, I do not meet many of the women he dates because you are the first one he has ever brought here. I just meant that he dates women who are beautiful like you and sure of themselves."

"The secret is not to let them see you sweat."

"What?" Lydia looked confused.

"People tend to take you at your own value." Ginny repeated a piece of advice she'd received when she'd first started to work. "If you act confident, people tend to believe you really are."

"Nobody believes me about anything." Lydia sounded resigned. "I thought I would walk with you down to the lounge. It will take Philip a few minutes to change."

So Philip was back! Ginny felt a frisson of excitement.

Suddenly the evening seemed brighter, full of possibilities
that it had lacked just seconds before.

"Thank you." Ginny smiled at Lydia. "That's kind of
you."

Lydia flushed. "I try to be a good hostess, what with
Philip caught up in that nasty labor dispute at the Athens
factory, and Jason behaving like..." Lydia clicked her
tongue in exasperation.

So Philip had gone somewhere on business. His absence
had had nothing to do with her. Ginny's spirits lifted even
further.

"I do not know why Jason is being so surly toward you.
It's none of his business that Philip and you..." Lydia gestured impotently.

"Will anyone else besides the Stavrinidises be coming?"
Ginny changed the subject. Jason Papas's part in this affair
was not something she wanted Lydia curious about.

Lydia shrugged. "Not unless Jason invited someone at
the last minute, which I doubt. I think Jason issued the
invitation in the first place to try to give Julia a chance to
captivate Philip. Not that she ever could. She never talks
about anything but her hair and her clothes and who is
doing what to whom. Philip hates gossip. And while he
wants a woman to look good, he doesn't want to hear about
the effort it took."

Ginny chuckled at Lydia's tart tone. There was far more
to Lydia than first met the eye. If she could just escape
from Jason's stifling presence and Philip's overprotective-
ness.... No, Ginny hurriedly pulled her thoughts up short.
Lydia wasn't her problem. Beth was, and Beth's best interests conflicted with Lydia's.

"Julia and her parents have continued to hope," Lydia
continued, "because they know Philip has to marry someone, and Julia is suitable."

So was Creon, and look where that marriage had led! Ginny wanted to say, but she knew she couldn't.

"But now Philip has you." Lydia ended on a bright note as they entered a large formal sitting room Ginny hadn't seen before.

"Good evening." Lydia greeted the middle-aged couple sitting on the couch.

Surreptitiously, Ginny studied them. They reminded her of a type she saw often in her line of work. Wealthy, self-indulgent and convinced that the world had been created expressly for their benefit.

Mrs. Stavrinidis's supercilious stare did nothing to soften Ginny's first impression.

"And this must be Philip's...friend?" A voice from the corner caught Ginny's attention and she turned to find Julia Stavrinidis studying her with an intensity that bordered on being rude.

Lydia inched closer to Ginny as if to give Ginny moral support and said, "Ginny, this is Mr and Mrs. Stavrinidis and their daughter, Julia."

Ginny politely inclined her head.

There was a moment's embarrassing silence that Ginny made no effort to break. Finally, Mrs. Stavrinidis gave a grating titter and said, "You must tell us how you met Philip."

"I'll ask Philip to give you all the details if you're interested," Ginny said evenly.

"No, no," Mr. Stavrinidis said with a heartiness that didn't quite ring true.

"Are we going to meet your son?" Julia asked avidly.

"No, he isn't at his best at dinner parties," Ginny said. And if this is a sample of the conversation she's going to have to put up with, then she wasn't any too keen on them, either.

Lydia, ever the peacemaker, hurriedly asked Mrs. Stavrinidis a question about a mutual acquaintance, and the woman promptly launched into a rambling monologue.

Ginny pasted an interested expression on her face and retreated into her own thoughts. Thoughts of Philip and the feel of his body pressing her into the wet sand. The feel of his tongue touching her breast.

Mrs. Stavrinidis's sudden silence finally penetrated Ginny's erotic fantasies, and she looked up to see Philip's lean body in the doorway. Instinctively, her tongue slid over her lower lip and a warmth sparked to life deep in her abdomen.

Philip's disinterested gaze skimmed over the Stavrinidises and landed on Ginny. His breath caught in his throat when he saw the dress she was wearing. The deeply cut neckline exposed the swell of her breasts, and his fingers began to itch as he remembered the feel of her soft flesh. Hurriedly he lowered his gaze and found his eyes caught by the slender length of her legs encased in sheer black stockings.

A spurt of excitement slammed through him, tightening his body. Her legs looked so sleek and touchable. He wanted to run the palm of his hand over them. To slip his fingers beneath her skirt and find out if she was wearing stockings or panty hose. The knowledge that he couldn't filled him with a frustration. But he could touch her a little, he told himself. Enough to convince Lydia that he was the one who had been her lover.

"Good evening." Philip dropped the greeting into the silence as he walked toward Ginny, trying not to appear overeager. Perching behind her on the low back of the sofa, he gently began to caress her bare shoulder. Her skin felt smooth and warm to his touch, but not as warm as her breasts had felt.

A feeling of satisfaction curled through him as he felt her muscles tense beneath his caressing fingers. Ginny wanted his touch as much as he wanted to touch her. And that being the case, maybe making love to her wasn't such a bad idea. His entire body seemed to clench at the thought. After all, did it really matter that she'd been his brother-in-law's lover?

Yes, Philip admitted reluctantly. It mattered to him. But even knowing that, didn't extinguish his desire for her.

Deciding to worry about it later, he desperately tried to concentrate on what Mr. Stavrinidis was saying about the latest price of wheat imports. If he didn't get himself under control quickly, Ginny would realize just how much she was affecting him, and he didn't want her to know that. He wasn't even sure he wanted to know it himself.

Four

"Stop that!" Philip muttered under cover of kissing Ginny's cheek.

Stop what? His words echoed through her mind, finding no frame of reference to latch on to. She was too busy trying to block out the feel of his warm breath moving the tendrils of hair around her ear. It made her skin feel too tight. As if it couldn't contain the feelings burgeoning in her. As if they might burst out at any moment.

Her lips quivered at the thought of what her fellow dinner guests would do if she were to suddenly grab Philip by the lapels of his custom-tailored suit, pull him onto the couch and kiss him with the mindless abandon that she wanted to.

"It isn't funny," Philip hissed. "Stop shying away from me. We're supposed to be lovers."

Ginny moved her head slightly and found herself scant inches from the gleaming darkness of his eyes. They looked bottomless. As if she could tumble into them and never surface again. And hard. The reality punctured her dreamy state.

"Ginny, would you come with me to check on the babies while we are waiting for Jason to join us?" Lydia turned to Mrs. Stavrinidis. "If you do not mind?"

"Of course not," Mrs. Stavrinidis said.

Ginny hurriedly got to her feet. "Thanks for the timely rescue," she said once she and Lydia were far enough down the hallway not to be overheard.

Lydia sighed. "It is only a momentary respite. For both of us. What is the saying? A little of the Stavrinidises goes a long way. And with Philip behaving so strangely tonight…"

"What particular bit of strangeness are you referring to?"

Lydia gave her a long, thoughtful look. "You are not afraid of him, are you?"

Ginny blinked, taken aback by the question. She might be afraid of the way he made her feel, but not of what he might do. "Of course I'm not afraid of him."

"Julia is. She wants to marry his money, but she is frightened out of her wits by Philip."

"Maybe she knows something I don't," Ginny said flippantly, but Lydia ignored her.

"Most women never even see the man behind his money."

"That I find hard to believe!"

"It is true," Lydia assured her as they reached the nursery. As Ginny had expected, Damon was sound asleep and, after a brief word with Nanny, they headed back to the salon.

"And Philip acts very differently toward you." Lydia picked up their conversation. "I cannot ever remember him doing more than kissing a woman on the cheek in company. Yet tonight he cannot seem to keep his hands off you and, when he is not touching you, he is devouring you with his eyes.''

So Philip wasn't normally demonstrative in public? Ginny digested the information. So why was he making an exception for her? Because he didn't think that she deserved any respect and was subtly conveying his contempt to everyone?

No. She promptly discarded the idea. It didn't really fit what she knew of him. For one thing, she didn't think the man had a subtle bone in his body. For another, if that was his goal, it was obvious from the Stavrinidises' reactions that it wasn't working, and he could have seen that, too.

The most likely explanation was the obvious one. That he really was trying to convince the Stavrinidises that she was his lover. The fact that he was tormenting her in the process was probably just an unexpected bonus as far as he was concerned. He might even think that if he made her uncomfortable enough, she'd take Damon and leave.

But two could play Philip's game. Ginny's lips lifted in a wicked grin as she contemplated the possibilities. After all, he had said he wanted her to convince people that they were lovers, hadn't he?

''What are you planning?'' Lydia eyed her uncertainly.

''Just deciding the best way to give your brother what he wants,'' Ginny said blandly.

Lydia glanced upward, as if seeking divine intervention. ''And to think, just last week I was bemoaning the fact that nothing ever happens around this place.''

Ginny frowned. That was a strange thing for a woman to say who had just lost her husband a few months before. It's none of your business. Ginny pulled her thoughts up short. She had enough things to worry about without going looking for more.

"What took you so long?" Philip demanded the instant Ginny walked into the lounge.

"I'm so sorry." Ginny deliberately lowered her voice a pitch and hurried toward him as if she couldn't bear to be parted from him one second longer. A feeling of satisfaction filled her as she saw his eyes narrow suspiciously.

Taking a page out of Philip's manual on sexual frustration, Ginny perched behind him on the sofa so that she could touch him, and he couldn't retaliate.

"Every second I'm away from you seems like an eternity," she paraphrased an old song, feeling his shoulders quiver with suppressed laughter.

So he was amused, was he? She'd see just how amusing he found her efforts by the evening's end.

Reaching out, she slowly ran her fingertips along his jawline, savouring the feel of his muscles cording beneath her wandering touch. She pressed a little harder, exploring the sandpapery texture of his cheek. He must have to shave twice a day, she thought, because if he didn't he'd look like a pirate.

She stared blindly down at his dark hair as her imagination obligingly supplied an image of Philip with a short black beard and a loose white shirt with full sleeves ending in tight cuffs. He was standing on the deck of a triple-masted sailing ship, the brisk wind riffling his hair. Dreamily, her finger moved to trace over his ear. She barely noticed his convulsive jerk. She was too busy rearranging her fantasy.

No shirt, she decided. Pirates shouldn't wear shirts. She ran the tip of her tongue over her bottom lip as she visualized Philip without the shirt.

Her train of thought was derailed as Philip suddenly

caught her wandering fingers in his hand and held it captive against his shoulder.

Ginny simply used her other hand. Cupping his chin in the palm of her hand, she tilted his head backward and smiled down at him. A feeling of exhilaration surged through her at his frustrated expression. Philip might not like it, but for the moment he was in her power. It was a heady thought.

"Ginny!" Philip's voice was hard and tense. As if she'd wound him up too tightly for comfort, Ginny thought happily, wondering how long it would take until he surrendered. Or she did, she conceded wryly, because she was finding touching him a subtle torture also. She wanted to do much more than simply caress his face and neck. She wanted to make love to him. She squarely faced the fact. Even knowing that it was a very bad idea that would horrendously complicate an already complicated situation, she still wanted to do it.

"And how do you find Greece?" Mrs. Stavrinidis's voice was sharp, as if the sight of Ginny so casually caressing Philip was more than she could bear.

"Fascinating." Ginny gave the woman a meaningless smile as she slipped her forefinger beneath the collar of Philip's immaculate white shirt. "Absolutely fascinating," she groped for a sexy tone and must have found it because she could almost feel Philip's temperature rising.

"Ah, Jason, there you are." Mr. Stavrinidis greeted his host with obvious relief.

Under cover of Jason's response, Philip turned to Ginny and whispered, "Don't be so obvious!"

Ginny gave him a blank look as if she had absolutely no idea what he was talking about. Waiting until he turned back to the other guests, she leaned forward.

It was almost her undoing. His silky hair scraped eroti-

cally across the skin above her deeply cut bodice, short-
ening her breathing and sending a hectic flush over her
cheeks. What would it feel like to cradle his head against
her bare breasts? she wondered longingly.

"I've been making the acquaintance of your delightful
guest, Jason," Mr. Stavrinidis said. "She was telling us
what she thinks of Greece."

Jason stared at the man as if he'd made an off-color
remark.

"And its people." Ginny was unable to resist the gibe.
How dare that old tyrant stand there and act like an outraged victim when his precious son had caused this whole
mess?

"Somehow I missed lunch, and I'm starving," Philip
hurriedly injected into the sudden silence. "Is dinner ready
to be served?"

"Yes, we were only waiting for Jason," Lydia said.

"Damn right you should wait for me. It's my house,"
Jason snapped. Turning abruptly, he stomped toward the
dining room, followed more slowly by the rest of the party.

"What are you looking so pensive about, Miss Alton?"
Mr. Stavrinidis asked, and received a glare from his wife
for his curiosity.

"Hubris," Ginny said truthfully. "I was just wondering
how long a man would have to serve in purgatory for the
sin of hubris."

"Or a woman." Philip gave her a warning look.

"Ah, but excessive pride tends to be a masculine sin for
the most part. Don't you think so, Julia?" Ginny asked.

"Without a doubt," Julia agreed in heartfelt tones.

"Now, dear, you won't be wanting Philip to think that
you're..." Mrs. Stavrinidis's voice trailed off into silence.

"Philip knows Julia is a good girl," Jason said flatly.

Ginny bit her tongue to keep from retaliating. She knew

she wasn't going to change the way Jason thought about women and sex. Arguing with him would only embarrass poor Lydia who had the dubious honor of being the hostess of this group of social misfits.

Ignoring Jason, Ginny sat down beside Lydia and pulled Philip into the empty seat beside her. The rest of the party sank into chairs and then stared down at the exquisite place settings of porcelain, crystal and silver as if searching for a clue for their next step.

Ginny had no doubts about what she was going to do. She was going to continue her campaign of tormenting Philip. Under cover of the table, she slipped her shoe off and rubbed her toe across his ankle.

Philip jumped in surprise, knocking over his wineglass.

Ginny watched the dark red stain seep into the heavy cream damask tablecloth with pseudosympathy. "Don't let it bother you, Philip," she said brightly. "Everyone gets clumsy occasionally."

Philip gave her a glare that would have ignited paper at ten paces, and Ginny felt a momentary flare of nervousness. A nervousness she quickly stifled. All he could do was yell, and she didn't think there were any insults left that he hadn't already flung at her.

The maid hurriedly sopped up the mess and refilled Philip's wineglass before serving dinner.

Ginny picked up her fork and idly played with her food, not the least bit hungry. There wasn't room in her mind for such a mundane need as food. Not while Philip was so tantalizingly close.

Waiting until everyone was politely listening to Mr. Stavrinidis who was deep in an incomprehensible story about a business coup he'd just pulled off, Ginny insinuated her foot under Philip's pant cuff and rubbed the side of his calf. The thick hair on his leg scraped against her nylon-covered toes, creating a strange sensation deep in the pit of her stomach.

She wanted to touch more. She wanted...

Philip suddenly grabbed his wineglass and drained it.

Ginny raised her eyebrows in mock surprise and happily went back to exploring his leg with her foot. This was going to rank as one of her all-time favorite dinner parties.

By the time the Stavrinidises finally showed signs of leaving almost four hours later, Ginny was a tightly strung bundle of sexual frustration. She might have severely rattled Philip's self-control, but her efforts had definitely rebounded on her.

A hot shower is what was needed, she decided as she took advantage of the bustle of the Stavrinidises' departure to escape to the sanctuary of her room. Or failing that, a cold one. That might help to dissolve some of her tension. But even if neither worked, it had still been worth it to best Philip at his own game.

Not bothering to turn on the lights, she opened the drapes to allow the brilliant moonlight to flood the room and, grabbing her thin cotton nightgown that the maid had obligingly left near the foot of the bed, she headed toward the bathroom.

The shower didn't help. She still felt on edge and jittery. Emerging from the bathroom, Ginny crossed the moonlit room toward the bed, only to come to a startled halt when she saw Philip sitting on the edge of it. Her heart seemed to stop for a moment before it lurched into a rapid tattoo that echoed in her ears.

Ginny hurriedly pulled the drapes closed and flipped on the overhead light, hoping its brightness would dispel the intimacy of the darkness. It only made matters worse. With light, she could now clearly see Philip. He was wearing a snowy white, thick terry robe that highlighted his deep tan.

Her eyes dropped to his bare legs. He was obviously naked under the robe. Ginny desperately struggled to suppress her instinctive urge to yank his robe open and check for sure.

"What are you doing here?" She winced at the utter stupidity of the question, but at least his answer would fill a few minutes while she hopefully regained her normal competent manner. Not that she'd behaved in anything like a normal manner since she'd met Philip Lysander, she thought in despair.

Philip's lips lifted in a slow smile that sent a shiver of longing through her. "Responding to your invitation."

"I didn't issue any such thing! You told me to make them believe that we were lovers, and I did."

"And now I'm telling you we're going to make love."

Philip's calmly delivered words hit Ginny with the force of a blow, scattering all the very good reasons why they shouldn't. All that was left was her burning need to be closer to him. To touch him, to explore the mysteries of his body. To follow her desires to their natural conclusion.

Desperately fighting both herself and him, she took a deep breath, realizing her mistake when she saw his eyes widen as the thin cotton of her nightgown stretched tautly over her breasts. She resisted the urge to wrap her arms protectively around herself. She wasn't some naive little fool, she assured herself. She was a mature adult woman, who just happened to feel like a naive little fool.

"I don't take orders," she said. "Go away."

"Neither do I."

Ginny eyed him in acute frustration. She wanted him out of her bedroom, and she wanted him out now. While she still had a few remnants of her willpower left.

"You liked kissing me, didn't you?" Philip persisted.

Ginny briefly debated telling him no, but rejected the

idea for two reasons. First, Philip was far too experienced not to have read her reaction for the pleasurable response it was and, more importantly, it seemed like a betrayal of her basic self to deny what she really felt.

"Yes," she said defiantly. "So what?"

"So you'll like making love to me even more."

That I already know, she thought glumly. What I don't know is what I'll feel like afterward. When I start to think about my stupidity in getting mixed up with a man who doesn't even know who I really am.

"You don't understand," she muttered.

"Obviously, so come sit down and explain it to me."

I'd love to explain it to you, Ginny thought, if I just understood it myself.

Ginny sat down beside him, wanting the comfort of being close to him.

"Why are you making such heavy weather out of this?" Philip asked. "You are an experienced woman with a child. You obviously aren't averse to indulging your desires, nor do you seem to care about the conventions. So why not?"

Ginny felt discouragement slip over her like a silken gown, enveloping her in despair. How could her whole life have become such a complicated mess in such a short time? All she'd wanted to do was to help poor Beth obtain some peace of mind, and instead it was her own peace of mind that was being threatened. How could she fight Philip and herself? Her shoulders sagged under the weight of the problems that weighed them down.

She wanted to throw herself on the bed and indulge in a good cry. But modern women didn't give in to their frustrations, she told herself. They solved them. The knowledge didn't lighten her mood. She was fast coming to the conclusion that she was lacking a necessary component of the modern woman's makeup. They were supposed to be in control of their love life, and yet, with Philip, her reactions seemed to control her.

Philip watched her shoulders droop despondently. He wanted to take her in his arms and kiss away her fears. To tell her that everything would be all right. But the problem was that he didn't know that everything would be all right. He wasn't even sure that making love to her was such a good idea. And if he couldn't lay his own doubts to rest, how could he hope to settle hers?

Philip saw the quiver of her lower lip, and the impulse to cover it with his own was almost more than he could stand. He put his arm around her shoulders and, encouraged when she didn't push him away, gently tugged her closer.

He nestled her head beneath his chin, and the fragrant, flowery scent that clung to her skin teased his senses. She smelled so good, like springtime in London after the long dreary winter. Burying his face in her silky hair, he breathed deeply, allowing the scent to wash through him.

"It's all so complicated," Ginny muttered.

"No, it isn't." Philip tipped her head back against his shoulder and nuzzled the soft skin on her temple. His arms tightened instinctively as he felt her tremble. Why was she denying both of them what they wanted?

Could she be worried about Jason's refusal to acknowledge the boy as his grandson? But if she had just done a little more research about Greek families before she'd claimed Creon as the boy's father, she would have found out that Jason would hardly be likely to welcome her with open arms.

He brushed his mouth along the curve of her eyebrows, tracing over their length. Of course, Creon was probably the only man Ginny knew with very much money, he decided as he dropped feather-light kisses on her closed eyelids. A tingling sensation spread through him at the feathery feel of her thick eyelashes against his lips.

He had money. The thought surfaced through his be-mused sense of pleasure. Far more than Jason had. Enough money to indulge his every wish. Or Ginny's. He went back to nuzzling her temple, savoring her feminine scent. What would be the harm of providing for the boy himself? He admired Ginny's determination to secure her son's financial security, even if he didn't approve of the way she was going about it. Not only that, but if he were writing her support checks every month, it would provide a perfect excuse for him to continue to see her even after she returned to New York.

Perhaps if she weren't so worried about the boy, she could concentrate on other things. Like him and the fact that if he didn't make love to her soon, he was going to go stark raving mad.

"How much do you need for the boy?" Philip asked.

Ginny blinked and then blinked again as his words penetrated the sensual labyrinth that his wandering lips had plunged her into. A feeling of uneasiness slithered through her at the totally unexpected question. She stared up into his dark face, wondering what he was thinking. Could Jason have asked him to find out?

But if that were the case, why wait till now? Unless that was why he'd come to her bedroom in the first place, and the rest of his actions were simply a desire to pay her back for tormenting him earlier in the evening.

Ginny felt like screaming. It didn't seem fair that she should be landed with a whole new set of questions when she hadn't managed to answer the first set. Damon was why she had come to Greece in the first place, she reminded herself. Beth was counting on her to get Creon's family to recognize his son. And that being so, she couldn't ignore any overtures about Damon.

Taking a deep breath, Ginny said, "I think the best plan would be to find out the cost of a good private school, add

the expense of four years at a university to it and put te
percent over that figure in an investment plan designed t
be liquidated over a long period of time. Primarily in trea
sury notes, blue chip stocks and with a few bond marke
investments to offset the periodic volatility of the stocl
market.''

"Volatility?" Philip repeated, completely taken aback by
her words.

Ginny nodded. "I don't want to put all of Damon's fund.
in the stock market because you can lose a great deal o
your capital if you have to liquidate at any given time
Since the bond market tends to rise as the stock marke
falls, they offset each other.''

"Where did you learn about the stock market?" Philip
tried to reconcile her obvious financial expertise with th
fact that she was a kindergarten teacher.

"The financial markets have always been an interest o
mine," Ginny hedged. She gave him a level stare that dared
him to make some crack about grasping women. To her
relief, he didn't.

"What about the boy's living expenses?" Philip asked
Jason had said that she was demanding money, but he
hadn't said that all she was asking for was the boy's schoo
fees. If he really was Creon's son, why wasn't she asking
for more? A lot more. She would certainly be entitled to
it.

Ginny shrugged. "Damon lives with me. He doesn't eat
all that much, and his medical fees are covered by insur-
ance."

Now that sounded like the Ginny Alton he had come to
know. An independent woman capable of dealing with almost anything. But if that were the case, then why was she
asking for any money? A sense of frustration filled him
There was something wrong about this whole thing. Some-

thing that didn't quite ring true, and yet he couldn't put his finger on it.

"It would be easier to get the money out of me than Jason," Philip finally said.

Ginny felt an icy trickle of horror ooze through her. Surely Philip couldn't think that she was trying to trade sexual favors for money? "You better not be saying what it sounds like you're saying!" she bit out.

Philip stared at her for a puzzled moment and then his eyes suddenly widened as he understood. "You have a nasty mind!" he snapped.

"Forgive me. I guess I'm just not used to seeing you in the role of philanthropist." She defended herself, feeling considerably better at his honest outrage.

"I'm not a philanthropist, I'm a realist. And I want you away from Lydia. And the only way you're going to go is if you get what you came for. Besides, if the boy really is Creon's as you claim, then I'm a relative."

"Damon. His name is Damon," she muttered. "And your relationship to him is so slight as to be nonexistent."

"And I want to do it because people usually want to do things for their lovers," Philip added hopefully.

"You aren't my lover."

Philip gave her a crooked grin that tugged at her heart. "Hope springs eternal?"

Reaching into the pocket of his robe, he pulled out a small, flat packet and held it out to her.

Ginny stared down at the bright gold foil. He certainly came prepared. But while the condom would undoubtedly take care of any complications like Damon, it couldn't do a thing for all the underlying issues between them. Issues that Philip didn't even realize were there.

Ginny absently took the package and set it on the bedside table. But perhaps the fact that he didn't know that they existed was in her favor, she thought, trying to rationalize her growing need. Philip had accepted her as one person and he wanted to make love to that person. The fact that she was both more and less than what he thought was only a problem in her mind.

She sighed. What it all boiled down to was did she want to deal with her regrets of never having made love to Philip Lysander or did she want to deal with the complications that might arise if she did?

Ginny raised her eyes and stared into his night-dark eyes. In a strange way, she felt as if she'd known him forever. As if everything in her life to this point had merely been preparation for this man and this moment. As if she'd never be whole unless she experienced his lovemaking. Drawn by a need that defied rational logic, she slowly placed her hand over his and said, "I very much want to make love to you, Philip Lysander."

For a long moment he simply continued to stare at her as if lost in some dream of his own. Ginny wondered if he were seeing her or simply a willing woman in his bed. And she was willing, she made no attempt to lie to herself. She wanted this.

Raising his hand, Philip lightly ran his fingertip down the center of her forehead, over her nose to come to rest on her lips. Ginny shuddered as he lightly outlined them.

"You are a very beautiful woman, Ginny Alton."

"I know." Her words were muffled, as if she couldn't find enough air to fully form them.

Philip chuckled, and the warm rich sound teased her senses, making her want to snuggle closer. "What ever happened to a modest disclaimer?"

Ginny shrugged and the movement made her light cotton gown scrape over her breasts. They felt heavy, so incredibly hypersensitive that it was becoming difficult to concentrate on anything but how she felt and how soon she could feel even better.

"As our culture measures beauty, I am beautiful," she muttered distractedly. "It certainly isn't anything I can take credit for."

"And what can you take credit for?" Philip lowered his head and nuzzled the tender skin behind her ear. "Can you take credit for the fact that your skin is like velvet? Warm and soft and infinitely alluring. I want to explore every square inch of it.

"And your hair..." He stroked his hand over her shoulder-length hair, letting the strands slide between his fingers. "It's the perfect complement to your skin. Silky."

His fingers speared through it, and he tugged her closer, burying his face in her hair and breathing deeply.

"It smells so good. Like flowers. Wildflowers, I think," he murmured. "Because the scent isn't obvious. I have to get close to you to even smell it. And I want to get very close."

Ginny trembled as he rubbed his cheek over hers and the faintly raspy texture of his skin scraped enticingly across hers, emphasizing the tantalizing differences between them. Hinting at even more fundamental differences.

Blindly, Ginny turned her head, seeking his mouth. Her lips landed on the corner of his mouth, and she felt the rough warmth of his firm lips before they hungrily covered hers.

The pressure of his mouth sent a spurt of heat surging through her. A heat that threatened to burst into open flames when he shoved his tongue inside.

Ginny trembled as Philip explored the inside of her mouth, magnifying the need swirling through her. He tasted of Scotch and mint toothpaste and something else. Something infinitely alluring and totally unique. Something that came from the heart of his masculinity and that she could only sense, not clearly identify.

Hungrily, Ginny touched his face, running her fingers

over his cheek and feeling the faint tremor that rippled beneath his skin. That he felt such pleasure from her touch made her feel euphoric. Letting her hand trail downward, Ginny slid it between the lapels of his robe.

His dense body hair scraped over her palm and the shock of the feeling that poured through her held her motionless for a long moment.

"Don't stop," he whispered against her mouth.

"I'm not...I'm..." Ginny struggled through the maelstrom of sensuality to find words to try to express what she was feeling. She couldn't, and she finally gave up the effort as not worth the bother. Words were such imprecise things and so open to misunderstanding. Whereas feelings... She sighed happily.

Pushing her hand deeper into his robe, her probing finger discovered one of the flat nipples on his chest. Curiously, she explored it with her fingertip, and when she felt the shudder that rippled through him, she flicked her fingernail over the tight bud.

His arms tightened convulsively around her slight frame, and he pulled her down on the bed beside him. "You are the most incredible woman," he muttered against her mouth. "I want... I can't decide what I want to do first."

Ginny giggled. "Pick a number, any number."

"I think I got the gold ring," he said as he yanked his robe open and pulled her up against his bare skin.

The shock of feeling his hard muscles pushing into hers was electric. Ginny wiggled slightly, trying to intensify the sensations building in her.

To her disappointment, Philip pulled back. But before she could protest her loss, he began to fumble with the tiny buttons on the front of her nightgown. Finally, he managed to get her bodice open and, sweeping the edges apart, pressed her against his chest.

Ginny's breath escaped in a gasp as pleasure raced along

her nerve endings bringing them to life. Philip felt so...
Her thoughts suddenly dissolved into nothingness as he
moved, and his chest hair scraped across her sensitive nipples, making them ache unbearably.

She squirmed against him, beyond logical thought. Beyond anything but the need to sate the feeling growing in
her.

As if he shared her impatience, Philip gently pushed her
onto her back and groped for the condom she'd set on the
bedside table, fumbling to open it.

"You're the most intoxicating thing I've ever run
across," he muttered, and his voice echoed strangely in her
ears. It sounded deeper, huskier as if it were coming from
a great distance. "I don't know how long I can make this
last. I feel so..."

Ginny could feel his hot breath on her breasts, tightening
the sensitive flesh to tormenting levels. Suddenly his tongue
darted out, and he licked one nipple.

Ginny moaned in mingled pleasure and frustration. It
wasn't enough. Reaching for his head, she tugged him
down to her. As if to reward her initiative, his mouth closed
hotly around her nipple and he suckled.

"Philip!" Her voice was a sharp gasp of pleasure.

Grabbing the hem of her nightgown, he yanked it up to
her waist and slipped between her legs.

"I'm sorry," he gasped, "but I can't wait anymore."

A heavy throbbing sensation began to reverberate deep
in her abdomen, blocking everything but the need to satisfy
it. And Philip was the key. Ginny grasped his shoulders
and frantically dug her fingers into his firm muscles. His
skin felt hot. Hot and dry as if he had a raging fever.

Ginny tensed as Philip probed her moistness. His finger
suddenly slipped inside her and she instinctively lifted her
hips against his hand.

Her breath caught in her throat as she felt the hot, rigid

length of him pushing against her sensitive skin, demanding entry. Faster, she mentally urged him.

As if they were in mental union as well as physical, he suddenly thrust forward, burying himself deep within her. For a long moment, he held himself absolutely still as if savoring their contact, and then he began to move, stroking the throbbing intensity of her desire. Driving it higher and higher with each measured thrust.

Mindlessly, Ginny grasped his lean waist and arched into him. Her movement catapulted her over the edge of sanity into a world where nothing mattered but the urgent emotions that gripped her. Every muscle in her body clenched as Ginny spun through a sensual world composed of heat and color and pleasure too deep to be fully comprehended. Dimly, as if from a distance, she could feel Philip moving faster as he increased the rhythm of his thrusts until finally he grasped her buttocks and lifted her against his exploding body before he collapsed limply on her.

Ginny lay beneath him feeling totally relaxed and yet curiously alive. As if their lovemaking had opened new vistas in her mind that she hadn't even been aware of before.

She snuggled her cheek against his damp shoulder. She could hear the frantic thudding of his heart echoed in her own body. All she could think about was a commercial she'd once seen about how it didn't get any better than this.

Five

Ginny shifted restlessly as the morning sun shining in through the crack in the drapes nudged her awake. She stretched her legs toward the end of the bed as a languid feeling of intense satisfaction oozed through her like warm syrup. Deliberately she kept her eyes closed, not wanting to wake up and deal with the realities of the day. Not when her memories of last night were so fantastic.

Tentatively Ginny inched her foot toward the side of the bed, hoping to find Philip still there. If he were... The temperature of her body seemed to soar.

To her disappointment, Philip's side of the bed was empty. Which was probably for the best. She needed time to figure out what had happened before she faced him again. No, she corrected herself. She didn't need to figure out what had happened. She knew what had happened. She had made love to Philip and, in doing so, had redefined who and what she was. What she wasn't so clear about was why.

Nor did she have a clear idea of how Philip had viewed last night. Philip was a very sophisticated man. Maybe he hadn't found what they'd shared as unique as she had.

The weight of the cotton sheet covering her seemed to press down on her hypersensitive skin, intensifying her uncertainties. What if...

"Are you awake?" Philip's hard voice sliced through her muddled thoughts, jolting her to full awareness.

Ginny's eyelids flew open, and she saw Philip standing just inside her bedroom door. Eagerly her eyes skimmed over his face, looking for some sign that what they had shared last night had changed him.

A sinking feeling settled in the pit of her stomach at his implacable expression. He looked more like the Lord High Executioner than a lover.

Ginny resisted the impulse to wiggle farther down under the sheets. The fact that he was formally dressed in a light gray suit complete with white shirt and conservatively striped tie while she was entirely naked made her feel at a tremendous disadvantage, both mentally and physically.

"I want to talk to you." Philip broke the uneasy silence.

Ginny stared at him, her eye caught by the tiny muscle twitching beside his mouth. Don't let him spoil last night. She silently sent up a frantic prayer.

"I didn't want you to think that..." Philip gestured toward the bed.

Oh, I don't think at all, didn't you know? Ginny thought with savage self-derision. If I did, I never would have made love to you.

"What I meant... Lydia is my sister..."

Each word seemed to impact her flesh with the force of a blow, inflicting an individual bruise.

"Last night was just…"

Ginny swallowed the urge to scream at him to shut up. She knew she couldn't let Philip see how upset she was becoming because he'd realize how affected she had been by their lovemaking. He might try to use that knowledge against her in her fight to get Jason to recognize Damon as Creon's son. Or even worse, he might pity her. Her skin crawled at the thought.

"Why are you making such heavy weather of last night?" Ginny struggled to inject a flippant note in her voice. "It wasn't all that big a deal."

If it had been any bigger a deal, Philip thought, he might have exploded! Philip was inexplicably furious at the uncaring tone in her voice. And his anger added to his sense of confusion. His whole purpose in talking to her this morning was to make sure that she didn't try to use his mindless response to her against him. And yet her assurance that she didn't think their lovemaking was any big deal made him livid.

Frustrated, Philip shoved his fingers through his dark hair, disheveling it. This was what he wanted. He tried to hang on to the thought and blank out everything else. It was an impossible task with Ginny sprawled so seductively in the bed.

His eyes traced over the way her tousled blond curls were spilled across the white pillowcase before they dropped to her breasts, which were clearly outlined beneath the thin material. A jolt of desire tore through him, and he wanted nothing in the world so much as to walk across the room and pull that sheet down so that he could touch her.

When he felt himself actually taking a step toward her, his fear gained the upper hand, locking his muscles and holding him rigid. Helplessly, he stared at Ginny, feeling

as if he were suffocating. As if he would die if he couldn't
hold her in his arms. Now. His smothering sense of urgency
was a feeling that he'd never had before about a woman,
and he didn't want it. It weakened him. Weakened him and
made him dangerously vulnerable.

But only if Ginny knew about it, Philip rationalized. If
he were to just leave the room, she'd think that he didn't
place any more importance on what had happened last night
than she did. Taking a deep breath, Philip forced himself
to turn his back on the sensual picture she presented and
walk away. It was one of the hardest things he'd ever done,
and he found that he was damp with sweat by the time he
reached Jason's study.

Slumping down in the desk chair, Philip stared out the
French doors to the sea. The last thing he wanted to do at
the moment was to drive into Athens and deal with labor
problems. And that was exactly the reason why he should
do it, he told himself. His headlong response to Ginny Alton was no more than a temporary aberration and, while he
didn't begin to understand it, he had to neutralize it as soon
as possible. And the best way to do that would be to fall
back into his familiar routine.

Determinedly, he reached for the phone to call the factory and tell them he'd be in later that morning.

Ginny was equally determined to put her life back on its
normal even keel. Or at least try. Climbing out of bed, she
headed toward the bathroom.

You're a liberated woman. You know all about sex, she
told herself and then sighed despondently. The problem was
that what she'd shared with Philip went far beyond mere
sex. It was as if she'd suddenly discovered a whole new
way of experiencing sensation, and she had the disheartening feeling that she would never be quite the same again.

Ginny adjusted the flow of the shower and stepped beneath its stinging spray, trying to wash away the feel of Philip's hands and mouth on her skin. But she only had to close her eyes to relive the faint pressure of his lips moving across her skin.

Snap out of it! she ordered herself. She was in Greece to help Beth and Damon, not to indulge her own needs. She absolutely couldn't lose sight of her loyalties, because Philip wouldn't. Philip had made love to her, but as he'd been so quick to point out this morning, he hadn't forgotten where his priorities lay.

And neither would she. Beth's interests had to be her primary concern. But what were Beth's best interests? Ginny wondered as she climbed out of the shower and began to briskly dry herself with one of the thick white towels. Beth said she wanted Damon's education fees paid, and Philip had intimated that he might be willing to do that. Ginny forced herself to ignore her initial distaste of the idea and to consider it. Would Beth want her to accept Philip's offer?

Ginny slipped on her bright blue-and-green floral sundress and began to brush her hair. She wasn't sure. She knew that she herself wouldn't take money from Philip even if they hadn't complicated the situation with their lovemaking. Damon's education wasn't Philip's responsibility. It was Creon's, and since Creon was dead, that responsibility fell to Jason.

And not only that, but there was the larger issue of Jason recognizing Damon as his grandson.

Ginny sighed as she shoved her feet into her flat white sandals. She didn't know. Just as she didn't know if Beth would still want Jason to claim Damon once she found out that her precious Creon had had a wife and three children.

It was possible that Beth might want to wash her hands of the whole Papas family.

Ginny didn't even know if she should tell Beth about Lydia and the girls. Maybe the best thing to do would be to say nothing and leave Beth her illusions of an honorable Creon who had loved her.

But if she didn't tell Beth and Beth somehow found out on her own...

Ginny rubbed her forehead in frustration. So many what ifs and so few certainties.

"Honestly," Ginny muttered to herself as she hurried to the nursery to check on Damon, "your life is beginning to resemble a soap opera and a badly written one at that."

"Ah, good morning, Miss Alton." Nanny looked up from the rocker where she was giving Jasmine a bottle. "Damon is all finished with his breakfast and waiting for a cuddle from his mum."

"Thank you." Ginny reached down and picked up Damon, kissing his soft hair and taking a deep breath of his clean baby smell. "I'm sorry I overslept." She hoped that the flush she felt on her cheeks wasn't visible across the sunny nursery.

"The sea air affects lots of people that way," Nanny said comfortably. "And Mr. Lysander said you'd be a little late when he was here earlier to see the babies."

"Here?" Ginny blinked in surprise.

"Very fond of his niece, he is, and of course, Damon is..." Nanny's voice trailed away as if she didn't want to say what everyone believed. "He took Damon for a walk out along the shore while I was bathing Jasmine."

"I see," Ginny said, wondering what Philip was up to. Could he possibly be coming to believe that Damon really was Creon's son and, as such, was really a part of the family? Or could it be that he was merely trying to reinforce the idea that Damon was his? She didn't know, and asking Philip wouldn't get her any answers. Despite what they'd shared, his words this morning had left absolutely no doubt in her mind that nothing between them had changed with regard to Damon or Lydia.

Ginny strapped Damon into his infant seat, carried him over to the open French doors and looked out onto the terrace. In her present state of mind, she most definitely didn't feel up to another acrimonious exchange with Jason.

To her relief, the only person on the terrace was Lydia. She was seated at a table staring at a white square of paper. Curious, Ginny walked over and sat down across from her.

Lydia jumped at Ginny's appearance. She recovered quickly and said, "Good morning, Ginny. And a good morning to you, my handsome lad." Lydia smiled at Damon who burbled happily at her.

Ginny set Damon in his infant seat on the table and accepted the cup of coffee Lydia handed her. She added cream and sugar and took a reviving sip of the hot liquid.

Lydia looked back down at the square of paper, a frown on her thin face.

"Not bad news, I hope?" Ginny said.

"No," Lydia said slowly, as if she weren't any too certain of the fact. "It is an invitation. An invitation to a showing."

"A showing of what?"

Lydia nervously rubbed her fingers over the black print. "Art," she said. "In Athens tonight."

"Who by?"

"Someone I used to know." Lydia said softly.

"Steward Morris?" Ginny guessed.

Lydia flushed a painful red and then it faded, leaving her face abnormally pale.

"Yes, but he never... I never... He probably does not even remember me," Lydia muttered.

"He sent you an invitation," Ginny pointed out.

Lydia sighed. "Yes, but..."

"Art showings are fun." Ginny encouraged her. "Besides, seeing old flames can be very illuminating. Your Steward Morris could turn out to be a Johnny Amador."

Lydia looked confused. "I do not understand. Should I know this Johnny Amador?"

Ginny chuckled and handed Damon a teaspoon to play with. "Johnny Amador was a boy I went to high school with. I worshiped him from afar, but he was enamored of football and the head cheerleader, in that order."

"So what happened?" Lydia asked curiously. "Did he suddenly discover you?"

Ginny shook her head. "No, we both went off to college and I didn't see him again until our tenth-year class reunion."

"And this time he fell in love with you?"

"No. This time I took a good look at him. His hair was thinning, he was fifty pounds overweight and he chain smoked."

Ginny wrinkled her nose in self-derision. "Not even with my eyes closed could I regain a spark of what I had felt."

"And you think that is what will happen when I see Steward again?"

"Maybe. Maybe not. The point is that there is absolutely no reason why you shouldn't go to this showing and find out."

"Oh, yes there is! Philip would not like it."

"Stuff Philip!" Some of Ginny's frustration with him spilled over. "The man is your brother, not your keeper."

Lydia grimaced. "I know it, and you know it, but does Philip know it?"

"You could tell him after the fact," Ginny suggested, and Lydia looked intrigued.

"You mean just go? But what if something happens?"

"What could possibly happen?" Ginny asked. "You're a competent woman of the nineties. You've got better sense than to wander down dark alleys, haven't you?"

Lydia nodded slowly. "But even so... Ginny, would you come with me?"

"Me?" Ginny was taken aback.

Lydia nodded vigorously. "Everything seems so easy when you say it, but when I think about trying to manage it myself everything gets complicated."

Absently, Ginny smiled at Damon as she considered Lydia's plea for help. While she knew getting too involved with Lydia was not a good idea, attending one art show wasn't that big a commitment.

Added to which, going into Athens would allow her to distance herself from Philip for a while. After last night's lovemaking she was in very real danger of becoming obsessed with the man. Maybe going away for a day would help to put him into perspective.

"We could take the babies and Nanny with us and drive up this morning. Then this afternoon we could go shopping for something to wear and spend the evening at the showing," Lydia suggested tentatively.

"All right." Ginny tried to sound more enthusiastic than she felt.

Lydia's face lit up, and she grinned at Ginny, looking more carefree than Ginny had ever seen her.

"What are you two looking so pleased about?"

Ginny's stomach did a sudden flip-flop at the deep sound of Philip's voice. She hurriedly looked down as she struggled to get her chaotic emotions under control. Even after his humiliating attempt to draw back from her this morning, she still wanted to fling herself into his arms.

Philip glanced from the top of Ginny's down-bent head to Lydia's frozen expression.

"Was it something I said?" he asked.

Ginny forced herself to look at him. Whatever demons had been driving him earlier seemed to have been dispelled. He looked his normal self. Unconsciously, she relaxed.

Philip reached out and ruffled Damon's hair, then glanced at Ginny, his eyes instinctively homing in on her lips. The lipstick she was wearing gave them a slight shine. He wanted to taste it and see how it changed the basic scent and taste of her mouth. He wanted to keep kissing her until it was all gone.

He should kiss her, he rationalized. Lydia thought Ginny was the mother of his child. She would expect him to kiss Ginny good morning. He had an obligation to kiss Ginny.

Slowly, savoring the coming contact, Philip reached out and grasped the nape of Ginny's neck. A feeling of omnipotence surged through him as he felt her tremble. Her skin was warm, and the soft strands of her hair felt like the silken threads his mother used for her embroidery.

Unable to resist the lure of her lips a moment longer, he lowered his head and covered her mouth with his. Just a brief kiss, he told himself. Just long enough to convince Lydia that he and Ginny were getting along fine. Just...

His thoughts shattered, fragmenting into dozens of pulsating sensations. Pressing harder, his tongue darted out to taste her lipstick. Sexy, he thought foggily. Ginny tasted sexy.

His body began to tighten at the memory of her flowery perfume. At the memory of how it had smelled on the skin of her breasts. How it had been faint on the curves and more intense on the undersides.

All he wanted to do was to pull her into bed, kiss her senseless and then bury himself deep in her welcoming body. He wanted to hold her captive while he rocked back and forth, feeding his pleasure until it grew to fill his whole world.

The sound of Lydia clearing her throat dispersed the sensual fog he was drowning in. He regained his control and took a step back.

He looked down into Ginny's face. Her lips looked softer, fuller than they had. As if they had absorbed some of the passion that had been seething through him.

What was she feeling? he wondered uneasily. She seemed to enjoy kissing him just now, and her response last night had been everything he could have asked for, but was it real? Did she really like making love to him or was she simply faking it for reasons of her own. A flicker of doubt curled through him as he remembered his offer to pay for the boy's school fees before they had made love.

Never in his life had he felt uncertain about a relationship with a woman. He'd always been very clear about what he was willing to offer a woman. If she wasn't willing to accept his terms, he moved on with mild regret. But with Ginny everything was different, and he wasn't even sure why.

As if from a distance he heard Lydia saying something, and he gratefully turned to her, using the sound of her hesitant voice as a lifeline to pull him free from his disquieting thoughts.

"...and go shopping in Athens." The last part of Lydia's sentence finally registered in his mind. They were planning to go into Athens! Without him! He felt a cold chill of fear. Between Lydia's extreme reticence and Ginny's idiotic assumption that she could cope with anything, who knew what might happen to them. He couldn't possibly allow them to go by themselves. He'd have to go along and make sure they stayed out of trouble.

"I intend to drive back to Athens shortly. You can go with me," Philip said.

"With you?" Lydia mumbled. She shot an agonized look at Ginny that Philip missed as he took a swallow of Ginny's coffee.

Ginny tried not to let the sudden spurt of excitement she felt show. She should tell Philip he hadn't been invited because this was strictly a female party. She knew she should. It would be hard enough for Lydia to defy her family when Philip wasn't there. It would be almost impossible under his disapproving eye.

Not only that, but if Ginny were to ever be able to put her confused feelings for him into any kind of perspective, she needed to distance herself from him while she constructed some defenses against him. But even knowing all that, Ginny still couldn't bring herself to tell Philip he couldn't come. Not with the taste of him still on her lips. Not when her nerves still sang with the pleasure of having kissed him.

And it was Philip's apartment they were intending to use. They could hardly ban him from it. She then added the final and most compelling rationalization for her weakness. Besides, telling Philip what to do would be an exercise in futility. He hadn't listened to anything she'd said yet. There was no reason to think he meant to start now.

"But we're just going to go shopping," Lydia tried.

"I assumed that since you're both women."

"Careful, my friend. You're skirting dangerously close to male chauvinism," Ginny said.

"Since when is stating a fact male chauvinism?" Philip demanded.

"Taking the fact that two women intend to go shopping and generalizing it to the whole sex sure isn't logic," Ginny shot back.

"Logic! How can you talk about logic when you're being illogical?" Philip said.

"Umm, it really doesn't matter," Lydia offered tentatively.

"Of course it matters," Ginny told her. "If you and your sisters would have hauled him up short, years ago, he wouldn't have such insufferable views today."

"Insufferable!" Philip howled.

"He isn't always insufferable," Lydia said.

Ginny grinned at Philip's outraged expression. "Damned with faint praise."

"Do you have any sisters, Ginny?" Lydia asked.

"Nope, I'm an only."

"You poor thing." Lydia seemed honestly sorry for her. "You must have been very lonely."

"Not particularly," Ginny assured her. "And I did have…" She hurriedly caught herself before she mentioned Beth. That could lead to questions she didn't want to answer and not answering them might make Philip wonder why she didn't want to talk about her only cousin. And she most emphatically didn't want Philip wondering about Beth. If he were to find out that Beth was really Damon's mother… Ginny barely suppressed a shudder. Beth wouldn't stand a chance against Philip. His confrontational style would reduce her to tears in minutes.

"…a dog," Ginny hurriedly said as she realized they were waiting for her to finish her sentence. "I had a small spotted dog named Charlie."

"Dogs are not the same thing as having brothers and

sisters,'' Lydia said. ''You must make sure that you have some for Damon.''

Ginny gulped at the sudden flare of emotion that scorched over her nerves. Children? Hers and whose? Philip's? She glanced at him to find him staring at her with an unreadable expression on his dark face. What would their children look like? she wondered. He was so dark, and she was so fair. Would their colorings blend or would his darkness smother her fairness?

Much as her common sense was being smothered, she reined in her imagination. She was about as likely to have Philip's children as she was to fly. He might want to make love to her, but he wasn't interested in anything more permanent. And neither was she, she assured herself. Philip was not the type of man any sane woman married. He was a product of his culture every bit as much as she was of hers, and they really didn't mesh.

''You two go get ready while I bring the car around.'' Philip's voice sounded strange to Ginny's ears. As if it were slightly muffled.

''I'll tell Nanny,'' Ginny said. At the moment all she wanted to do was to escape from Philip's intent gaze. Picking Damon up out of the infant seat, she carried him back to the nursery and then went to her room.

Leaning back against her closed bedroom door, Ginny took a deep breath, trying to still her jumpy nerves. It didn't help, and she was starting to feel slightly desperate. Somehow she had to figure out a way to defuse her reaction to Philip before he realized just how intense it really was. Not only that, but it was extremely hard to live with. It was rather like dodging through rush-hour traffic—emotionally exhilarating, but potentially dangerous.

Ginny wandered over to her rumpled bed and sat down on it, intending to plan. It was a mistake. The bed smelled ever so faintly of the cologne Philip used. It reminded her of making love to him, and that effectively destroyed her ability to think clearly. With a sigh, she gave up and started to pack. She'd worry about logic later. For now, she might as well go with the flow and see where it lead. She shivered in sudden anticipation. With luck it might well lead her back into Philip's bed.

The drive into Athens quickly took on all the charms of a prolonged session with the Spanish Inquisition. At least as far as Ginny was concerned. Nanny sat in the back between the two infants in their car seats, while Lydia and Ginny shared the front seat with Philip.

Lydia, no doubt thinking she was being tactful, had pushed Ginny into the middle next to Philip. Ginny knew it was a bad idea to spend the hour-and-a-half trip in close proximity to Philip, but even knowing it, wasn't enough to make her refuse. She craved contact with him, no matter what the consequences.

By the time they had reached the main highway, Ginny was a bundle of nerves from the hard pressure of Philip's thigh brushing against her leg. She felt like a woman dying of thirst who was standing knee-deep in water and couldn't bend down to drink. And as if that weren't bad enough, Damon began to cry in a heartbroken manner that made Ginny feel slightly desperate.

"Maybe I could hold him..." Ginny began.

"No." Philip flatly vetoed the idea. "The boy stays in his car seat. If something happened, you couldn't hang on to him. He'd hit the windshield."

Ginny sighed, knowing Philip was right, but it was cold comfort. Damon sounded so miserable. As if he'd lost his last friend in the world.

"If he doesn't quiet down shortly, we'll stop for a cool

drink and you can try feeding him," Philip said. "Some
real food might be nice."

Lots of things would be nice, Ginny thought dispiritedly
Damon having his mother here, for one. Or her not behaving like a lovesick adolescent over Philip, for another
Ginny sighed, and to her surprise, Philip removed a hand
from the wheel and patted her knee comfortingly. He was
such a surprising combination of contradictions, she
thought. She would have expected him to be angry at all
the noise Damon was making, but he wasn't. He was even
willing to alter his schedule to try to comfort him.

Thirty nerve-wracking minutes later, Philip pulled into
the dusty parking lot of a bustling restaurant.

Ginny hastily scrambled out of the car and unfastened
the still-crying Damon from his car seat, cradling his hot
sweaty little body against her shoulder.

"There, there, sweet'n," Ginny crooned to him.

Damon gave her an indignant look, added a few final
howls as if to tell her that he wasn't impressed and then
closed his eyes and fell asleep.

"Poor mite." Nanny smiled at him. "He's worn himself
out."

"To say nothing of the rest of us," Philip said dryly
"Since we've already stopped, we might as well get something to drink."

Ginny followed Philip, Lydia, Nanny and Jasmine into
the restaurant, looking around the dusky interior as they
waited for someone to seat them. She felt a quick surge of
excitement as she saw the public phone on the far wall.

Perfect, she thought. She could use it to call Beth and
give her a report on Damon. There was no way that Philip
could trace a call made from a public phone even if he
should wonder who she was calling.

Ginny waited until the waiter had settled them into an

empty table near the front and then said, "I want to make a call. I won't be a second."

"A call? To whom?" Philip frowned at her.

Ginny ignored him as got to her feet, being careful not to wake Damon. Beth would hardly be likely to believe that he was fine if she could hear him screaming in the background.

"You didn't answer me," Philip said.

Ginny smiled limpidly at him. "Simply because someone asks an impertinent question doesn't obligate me to answer it." She ignored both Nanny's widened eyes and Lydia's gasp. Honestly, Ginny thought in exasperation. No wonder Philip was so autocratic. He never met any opposition.

"Order me a lemonade, please," Ginny said, and hurried over to the phone before someone else decided to use it.

Philip watched as Ginny waited for her call to be connected. From the amount of time it took, she was undoubtedly calling someone back in the States. But whom? Damon's real father? A lover? A gust of anger battered his composure. He didn't want to think about her making love to another man. It made him feel faintly murderous.

But whomever it was she was talking to, it was someone that she was very fond of, he decided. He took a drink of his coffee, trying to ignore the dark feeling of rage that bubbled through him at her softened expression. She didn't look like that when she talked to him. Although she did when she muttered nonsense to the boy. She obviously loved the boy. Did that mean that she loved the man she was talking to? He didn't know. He only knew that he found the idea entirely unacceptable.

Philip stared blankly down into the black depths of his coffee. He'd always thought that jealousy was the mark of a man who had no self-control, and now to find out that he felt that way about Ginny... He shoved his fingers through his hair in frustration. How could his calm, ordered life have gone to hell so completely in just a few days? More to the point, what could he do about it?

Looking back at Ginny, he winced at the tender smile that curved her lips in response to something the man at the other end of the line had said. He wanted to grab the phone out of her hand and hang it up. He wanted to take her in his arms and kiss her so thoroughly that she wouldn't even remember whom she'd been talking to.

He grimaced at the thought of what the restaurant's patrons would say if he were to actually do it. More importantly, what would Ginny do? Would she kiss him back or would she yell at him? He didn't know. But he did know that whatever course she decided on, she'd throw her whole heart into it. She wouldn't sulk in offended silence like most women. Ginny told you exactly what she thought. You didn't have to guess.

Later, he comforted himself. Once they reached the apartment, he'd make some excuse to get her alone and he'd kiss her senseless. But he wouldn't mention the phone call. Letting her know that he resented her calling another man would give her a lever to use against him.

Six

"Nap time, angel." Ginny dropped a kiss on Damon's warm cheek, and he gave her a sleepy smile in response.

Maybe now he could finally kiss her, Philip thought with a seething impatience he was finding harder and harder to disguise. He craved physical contact with Ginny but it was hard to find a way to be alone with her here at the apartment. All he needed was a kiss or two to last him until tonight when he could hopefully make love to her again.

"I'll help you with the boy," Philip said hurriedly when Lydia got to her feet, obviously intending to accompany Ginny to the nursery. As he'd hoped, Lydia smiled at him in approval at what she thought was his show of paternal interest and sat back down.

Philip felt a twinge of guilt at Lydia's expression, which he told himself was ridiculous. The boy wasn't his. He didn't owe the child anything. Even if Ginny accepted his offer of financial support, he still didn't intend to become personally involved with the child.

Although... Philip frowned as a feeling of uncertainty seeped through his mind. If Creon really had been his father, then who was going to play the part of male role model for the boy? A boy needed a man to tell him how to deal with the world. A mother couldn't explain about women and sex and business. For that, a boy needed a father.

Philip shut the nursery door behind them and pushed in the lock on the door. Nanny was still in the living room with Jasmine and Lydia. With luck, she'd stay there for another ten minutes or so.

He could almost feel his blood pressure rise as he watched the slow, sensual sway of Ginny's hips as she carried Damon over to one the cribs. Every time he saw her move, he was reminded of honey pouring out of a jug. And every time he watched her, his reaction was stronger and more urgent.

Philip moved closer to her as she tucked a light cotton blanket around the baby. When she had finished, he reached down and freed Damon's arms.

"Why did you do that?" Ginny asked.

"I hate to have my arms covered," he said. "The boy might not like it, either."

Ginny considered it a moment and decided that it wasn't worth arguing about. She was far more interested in why he had followed her into the nursery. A quiver of anticipation shot through her. Could he have wanted a moment of privacy to kiss her or merely to reassure Lydia that he was interested in his supposed son?

Ginny suppressed a sigh. How could she be so deeply involved with this man and yet be so unsure of his motivations? Or her own, come to that.

"Why did you come in here with me?" She decided the best way to find out would be to just ask.

Caught off guard by the directness of her question, Philip looked at her. There was a thin worry line between her eyes that he wanted to erase. He wanted to cover every inch of her face with kisses before he moved elsewhere. But he didn't have that much time, he reminded himself. He had to hurry.

Allowing his growing need to engulf him, he moved closer. He could smell the flowery perfume she favored as well as the very faint smell of baby powder. He felt his gut clutch convulsively. He'd never thought that the smell of baby powder was seductive, but suddenly he wasn't so sure.

Philip reached for her and, when she made no effort to evade him, pulled her up against him, his need making his movements clumsy. Feeling as if he were starving for the taste of her, he captured her lips. Her mouth was warm and tasted ever so faintly of lemonade. Slightly tart, like her personality. Savoring the taste, he lightly ran the tip of his tongue across her lower lip. His arms tightened as he felt the tremble that shuddered through her. Her susceptibility to his lovemaking gave him a euphoric feeling of power. As if he could do anything.

Eagerly he shoved his tongue between her lips, and the illusive taste of lemon intensified. He wanted more. His hands slipped lower to cup her soft hips. Lifting her, he held her tightly against his throbbing manhood.

He felt his mind begin to blur. He wanted to sink into the exquisite sensations engendered by their contact. He wanted to feel her bare skin against his. Slipping his hand into the bodice of her sundress, he rubbed his palm over her nipple, feeling it harden. It felt...

"Miss Alton?" Nanny's voice jarred his intense self absorption.

Philip raised his head and stared down at Ginny's flushed face. She looked like he felt—totally absorbed by the incredible pleasure that they seemed to so effortlessly generate between them.

A muffled sound of yearning escaped her, and it was almost more than he could bear. Forcing himself to step away from her, he hurried toward the door and unlocked it.

"Sorry," Philip told Nanny. "The door must have caught when I closed it."

If Nanny had any doubts about his explanation, she kept them to herself. She merely nodded and carried Jasmine over toward the empty crib beside Damon.

Frustrated, Ginny watched Philip leave, her body a seething mass of unfulfilled need. She hoped he didn't realize just how much she was coming to crave his kisses. For that matter, she didn't want to know it herself. It pointed to all kinds of future problems for which there were no solutions.

No. Ginny hurriedly pulled her fears up short. She absolutely refused to spend what little time she did have with Philip, worrying about things she had no control over. She'd simply take events as they came and extract the maximum amount of enjoyment out of them.

"Now don't you worry," Nanny said. "You go shopping with Mrs. Papas, and I'll take good care of the lad for you."

Ginny blinked and slowly focused on Nanny's bright face. A guilty flush stained her cheeks. Damon had been the last thing on her mind, and he should have been the first.

"Thank you," Ginny murmured and hurried out into the living room, hoping that Philip would be there so she could take one last look at him before she and Lydia left.

A feeling of pleasure shot through her at the sight of Philip sitting on the couch talking to someone on the phone.

"Ready to go?" Lydia asked.

Ginny reluctantly allowed her eyes to slide away from Philip, and she turned to Lydia. She looked far more animated than Ginny had ever seen her. Anticipation over seeing her old boyfriend had lent a sparkle to Lydia's dark eyes and a becoming flush to her normally sallow cheeks.

"Just a minute, Lydia," Philip said. "I want to get the latest update on the labor problems at the factory."

Ginny blinked. Philip was planning on coming with them? She shivered in anticipation at the thought of spending a whole afternoon in Philip's company.

"Did you ask him to come?" Lydia whispered to Ginny.

Ginny shook her head. "He probably just wants to..." Her voice trailed away as she realized that she had no clue as to why he was coming. She'd have staked a considerable sum on the fact that Philip was not the kind of man who would enjoy a leisurely afternoon examining the shops. Or for that matter, even tolerate it.

"Don't look so worried," Ginny whispered to Lydia. "We aren't going to meet anyone he won't like while we're out this afternoon, and maybe he'll be so bored that he'll go off on his own this evening."

Lydia immediately brightened, and Ginny felt a little freer to relish her own pleasure at the upcoming afternoon.

Unfortunately, her pleasure didn't last past their first stop, an exclusive salon filled with very expensive dresses. Lydia immediately plunged into the racks of clothes determined to find exactly the right dress to wear to the art show that evening.

Ginny duly admired the dresses Lydia held up for her inspection, but she didn't really care for Lydia's choices. She much preferred starkly classical lines for her evening wear and not the lacy, frilly, stereotypically feminine gowns that Lydia favored.

"That one would look good on you, Ginny. Try it on." Philip pointed toward a soft pink dress with a profusion of ruffles on a mannequin to their right.

"Too fussy," Ginny dismissed it.

"Women's clothes are supposed to be that way," Philip insisted. All of his friends' wives wore dresses like that. Only his business colleagues dressed like Ginny, and she wasn't a business colleague. She had a much different role in his life.

"And far too expensive," Ginny added, not wanting to get into an argument of what women were supposed to look like. She didn't want to hear about one more area in which she fell short of his ideal of womanhood.

"I'll pay for it, of course," Philip assured her, but Ginny didn't feel the least bit reassured by his offer. She felt hurt and angry. As if he were offering her payment for having made love to him.

"There is no 'of course' about it!" she hissed at him. "I pay for my own clothes, and don't you forget it!"

"But I want to buy it for you," Philip insisted. "You can't afford it."

Ginny glared at him in frustration, knowing that she could afford anything in the shop and also knowing that she couldn't tell him that. She was supposed to be a teacher, and everyone knew that teachers' salaries didn't run to designer clothes.

"I don't want it!" she snapped, and then hurriedly smoothed out her expression when she saw a salesperson glance their way. The woman took a step toward them, caught the expression on Philip's face and hastily retreated.

"Stop bullying the staff!" Ginny ordered.

"I never said a word to her!"

"You didn't have to. The poor soul probably knows you by reputation."

"I am a very reasonable man!"

Ginny snorted. "And pigs fly."

"Dammit, woman, all I want is to buy you something."

"And all I want is for you not to buy me something," Ginny shot back.

Philip stared at her, a dark flush of impotent frustration burning across his cheekbones. "You are the most infuriating woman...."

"I could say the same thing about you, but I'm far too polite."

"I am not a woman!" He seemed to take a great deal of pleasure in pointing out her lapse in grammar before he turned and walked out of the store.

"What is wrong with Philip?" Lydia asked as she watched him disappear into the crowd outside on the sidewalk. "Did he suddenly remember that he hates to shop?"

"Does he?" Ginny asked curiously.

"He avoids it like the plague. I thought he only came this time because of you. He certainly did not do it because of me."

"I think he came for reasons of his own," Ginny said. "And he left because I wouldn't let him buy me something."

"Oh, I see," Lydia said, obviously seeing nothing of the sort. But to Ginny's relief she dropped the subject.

"Never mind." Lydia patted Ginny's arm comfortingly. "We will have more fun without him."

Ginny firmly squelched her doubts and sat down in an empty chair while Lydia went back to searching for the perfect dress. Almost immediately, Ginny's thoughts turned to Philip and she fell into a delightful daydream in which they were lying naked on the beach with the sun gently warming their bare skin and the soothing water pulsing gently over their bodies.

She tried to imagine Philip smiling at her with a besotted expression on his face, but her imagination simply wasn't equal to the task. She could envision passion and anger, but Philip in the guise of besotted lover seemed almost a contradiction in terms.

What kind of woman would get a reaction like that from him? Ginny wondered. Someone who said yes and amen to his every pronouncement no matter how inane it was?

"What do you think, Ginny?" Lydia's hesitant voice interrupted her speculation.

Ginny looked up to see Lydia wearing a dark coral dress with a great deal of lace around the high neckline. That much lace, even when it looked to be handmade as this did, didn't appeal to Ginny, but somehow it suited Lydia.

"Very nice. It's sexy in a refined, ladylike sort of way." Ginny praised. "You'll knock his socks off."

"Do you really think so?" Lydia asked wistfully.

"You look great in that color." Ginny automatically tried to bolster Lydia's morale. "It puts a glow in your cheeks."

"Then I will get it. What are you going to wear tonight?"

"The dress I wore last night is the only one I brought that would be suitable, although..."

Ginny looked back at the dress Philip had liked and barely suppressed a shudder. There was no way she could wear that, but maybe she could find something that would appeal to Philip's taste while not totally offending her own.

"Why don't you buy something," Lydia urged. "Philip's favorite color is a light blue. Like that one over there."

Lydia pointed toward a dress on a mannequin on the other side of the showroom.

Ginny walked over to it, trailed by the helpful Lydia. The color was pretty, Ginny conceded. It reminded her of the early springtime sky and robins' eggs. And the material was good. She reached out and fingered the soft velvety texture of the silk. And it didn't have too many ruffles. Ginny eyed the one around the deeply scooped neckline.

"The neckline is a little low," Lydia murmured, "but you've got the build to carry it off."

"I'll try it on," Ginny decided. As long as she were the one paying for it and not Philip....

Ginny slowly smiled as an idea occurred to her. Maybe she could show Philip how she had felt by turning the tables on him. By buying him a piece of clothing. But what? she wondered as she carried the gown into the dressing room. Certainly not a tie. Ties were too impersonal and underwear was too obvious. So what...

A swimsuit, she thought. She'd buy him a sexy swimsuit. An anticipatory smile curved her lips. And when he complained, she'd say that she was just trying to copy his way of doing things.

Even though the rest of the afternoon seemed to drag without Philip, Ginny was very careful not to let her boredom show because Lydia was clearly enjoying herself.

When Lydia decided to finish her shopping by getting her hair styled, Ginny got the name of a men's shop from Lydia and went to buy Philip a swimsuit.

She found the shop without any trouble and walked in, pausing just inside the door to allow her eyes to adjust to the dimness after the brilliant sunlight outside.

"How may I be of service, madam?" an elderly man inquired in an impeccable English accent.

Ginny smiled at him, amused at the fact that he'd so quickly sorted out her nationality. "I want to buy a swimsuit."

"Ah, madam, I deeply regret that we only sell men's clothing." He looked as if the news were a blow to him personally.

"I know that. I want a man's swimsuit. For my..." Ginny paused, trying to decide what to call Philip. He was far more than a friend and also far less. "For a gift," she finally said.

"Ah, yes." The man brightened. "Of course. What size is the man you are purchasing it for."

Ginny felt a flush burn across her cheeks as her mind replayed an image of a naked Philip bending over her, his body swollen with the strength of his passion. Hurriedly she tore her mind away from its erotic thoughts and focused instead on his waist size.

"Well," she murmured, "he isn't fat and he isn't skinny. He's kind of..." She gestured with her hands.

The man took a deep breath as if prepared to endure and said, "If he normally shops here, we would have his measurements on record."

It was worth a try, Ginny thought. Lydia might have sent her here because this was where Philip bought his clothes.

"I don't know if he does, but his name is Philip Lysander," Ginny said hopefully.

Ginny watched in amazement as the man's face took on a reverent expression.

"Of course we have Mr. Lysander's measurements. We have made his suits since he first started wearing long pants. I will check his size. Please wait here."

Ginny blinked, trying to imagine Philip in short pants. She smiled as the image of a small boy with skinned knees and a carefree grin formed in her mind. Philip as a child must have been a constant challenge to his mother's peace of mind. Would his own children be like him? she wondered. Or would they take after their mother. A warm melt-

ing sensation flowed through her as she pictured a small
girl with Philip's dark hair and eyes and her more restrained
approach to the world.

"Madam?" The clerk's resigned tone was Ginny's first
hint that this probably wasn't the first time he'd spoken to
her.

"Yes?"

"This suit is similar to ones that we have sold Mr. Lysander in the past." He held up a navy boxer style suit.

Ginny shook her head in emphatic rejection. "That's not
at all what I had in mind."

"But it is what Mr. Lysander prefers," the clerk pointed
out.

"But since I'm buying it, it's what I prefer that's relevant. Why don't you show me what else you have."

The clerk sighed and gestured for her to follow him. He
led her toward the back of the store to a table filled with
swimsuits.

Ginny's eye was caught by a minuscule Lycra suit with
a large bull's eye painted on the front. She was tempted,
but she finally decided that she was trying to subtly make
a point, not bludgeon him with it.

The clerk noticed her interest and seemed to quiver in
revulsion. "We stock those for the tourists. Our regular
clients never buy them."

Ginny didn't bother to respond, although from the sound
of things, his regular clients could do with a little lightening
up.

A brilliant neon pink, Lycra racing suit caught her eye
and she picked it up, trying to imagine Philip wearing it.
The color would look spectacular against his heavily tanned
skin and the cut... Her breathing developed a hitch as she
tried to imagine the thin material stretched across his swollen manhood.

"The color is very…bright," the clerk finally said.

"I noticed," Ginny replied. "I love it."

The clerk heaved a sigh and gave in. "I'll wrap it for you. Please remember that if Mr. Lysander doesn't like it you may return it."

Ginny grinned at the man. "I'll also tell him that you tried to talk me out of it."

The man smiled back. "Thank you, but Mr. Lysander wouldn't blame me for selling it to you. He knows all about women."

Oh, he does, does he? Ginny felt a sudden flash of anger. How widespread was Philip's womanizing if even the clerks in the stores knew of his success with the opposite sex.

"Yes, indeed," the clerk continued as he processed her credit card. "I remember when his father used to bring him into the store when he was just a lad. He used to say that he loved to come here because his sisters couldn't."

Ginny felt her anger fade. Although she wasn't sure that she agreed that Philip knew all that much about how women thought. Greek women maybe, but definitely not American ones.

Lydia was waiting in the lobby of the hair salon when Ginny returned and, other than a curious look at the sack Ginny was carrying, Lydia didn't mention it. Ginny was grateful. Even though it was just a swimsuit, it was somehow private. Just between her and Philip.

Lydia spent the taxi ride back to Philip's apartment alternating between excitement at the upcoming evening and fear of what might happen if Philip were to find out about the art show.

Ginny simply listened, knowing that Lydia needed to verbalize her fears in order to confront them.

Shortly before dinner, Philip returned from wherever

he'd gone after he'd left them so abruptly that afternoon. From her vantage point behind the half-open nursery door, Ginny watched him pause just inside the door and check the mail sitting on the table in the foyer. He looked exasperated, tired and completely fed up. But fed up with whom? Her? A frisson of pain sliced through her as she considered the idea before rejecting it. His present mood couldn't be a holdover from this afternoon. She'd seen absolutely no sign that Philip brooded.

Her breath caught as he turned and headed toward the nursery. Quickly she skipped back from the crack in the door, not wanting him to know that she had been watching him.

He pushed open the door and strode over to Damon's crib where he stared down at the sleeping baby.

"Good evening," Ginny said. "If you're looking for Lydia, she's getting dressed."

He jerked around at the unexpected sound of her voice and stared at her, his eyes lingering on the soft, flowing lines of the dress she was wearing. A feeling of satisfaction heavily tinged with uncertainty filled him. Ginny had to have bought that dress after he'd left the store. To please him. So why wasn't he pleased? He liked the dress, but somehow it didn't suit her as much as he'd expected. She'd looked better in that black dress she'd been wearing last night.

"I'm glad you changed your mind," he finally said. "Get the bill for the dress and bring it to me in the study. I have to make a phone call before dinner."

Ginny watched him leave, torn between a desire to yell at him and an equally strong desire to give him the swimsuit she'd bought and let him see how it felt to be on the receiving end of someone's largesse.

Give him the suit, she told herself. It comes under the

heading of one patronizing gift being worth a thousand shrieks.

Hurrying back to her bedroom, Ginny grabbed the sack from the men's store and sped across the living room to Philip's study. She didn't want to waste a single minute. At best, her time with Philip would be short. As late as it was, Lydia would want to serve dinner as soon as she realized Philip was back. And after dinner, she and Lydia would be going to the art show.

Opening the door to his study, Ginny slipped inside and closed it behind her. Philip was sitting at a massive mahogany desk, talking on the phone in Greek. And from the furious expression on Philip's face none of the more polite phrases she'd learned were applicable in this situation.

Ginny watched as a muscle in his cheek twitched, and his grip on the phone tightened, whitening his knuckles.

Setting the sack on the edge of his desk, Ginny walked around behind him, placed her hands on his shoulders and rubbed her thumbs over the muscles at the base of his neck. He wasn't just tense, he was practically rigid. He needed to relax. To let go of the tension that was tying him up into knots. And she, as a graduate of her local Y's therapeutic massage course, was just the one to help him do it.

Ginny reached around him and tugged at the knot on his tie, finally freeing it. Carefully, so as not to distract him, she pulled it off and tossed it onto the desk. Savoring the feeling of power that undressing him gave her, she undid the first few buttons on his shirt and slipped her hand beneath his shirt collar. A sudden shock of pleasure at the feel of his body gave her pause.

Philip tilted his head back and stared at her for a long moment. Then he covered the receiver of the phone and muttered, "I'm busy."

"And very tense," Ginny told him. "You need to relax. Just ignore me."

Philip grimaced, but he didn't tell her to stop, so Ginny positioned her hands at the base of his neck as she'd been taught and began to knead his knotted muscles. His skin felt warm and supple beneath her fingers. And infinitely intriguing. Leaning forward slightly, Ginny breathed deeply of the scent of soap and cologne and sun that clung to him. He smelled so wonderful, she thought dreamily. Like distilled masculinity and power and long, love-filled nights. She closed her eyes the better to concentrate on the fantastic sensation.

"What are you doing?" Philip's voice was muffled.

Ginny forced opened eyelids that felt weighted, and peered down at him. He'd hung up the phone and she hadn't even noticed, she realized in shock.

Hastily she stepped back. "Trying to soothe your tense muscles," she said, hoping she sounded more self-possessed than she felt.

Philip gave her a grin that sent her heartbeat into overdrive. "I have a much more reliable method for doing that."

Ginny tried to ignore the flush she could feel heating her face. She wasn't some shy little virgin to be sent into a confusion by a sexual innuendo. Especially not when she'd like nothing better than to follow through on his suggestion. But not now. She clung to her original purpose and reached for the bag from the men's store.

"I bought you something." She handed it to him.

"A present? For me?" Philip asked uncertainly as if it were a concept he hadn't as yet encountered.

Ginny watched as he reached into the bag and pulled out the swimsuit. The minuscule bit of pink Lycra dangled from his tanned fingers.

"It's a swimsuit," she told him, trying to focus on why she'd bought it and not how he'd look in it.

Philip gave her a thoughtful look that made her uneasy. He wasn't reacting at all the way she'd expected. Instead of being annoyed at her buying him something so blatantly sexist, he seemed to be intrigued.

"Thank you," he said. "I'll have to take you swimming so you can see it on."

Ginny blinked, wondering if he really intended to wear it in public. Or if she wanted him to. Philip in that suit was her own private fantasy. Not one to be shared with any woman who happened to be passing on the beach.

"And you haven't yet told me how much you paid for your dress," he continued.

Ginny opened her mouth and then closed it in impotent frustration. Somehow he'd completely turned the tables on her, and she wasn't sure how. His gracious acceptance of her gift made her own refusal to accept the gift of a dress from him seem churlish. And yet she knew that it was different. She just wasn't sure how.

To Ginny's relief, Lydia suddenly pushed open the study door and said, "Dinner is ready."

"Coming," Ginny muttered, using dinner as an excuse to escape. She needed to think about what had happened, and she couldn't do it while staring at Philip holding on to that scrap of pink Lycra.

Dinner was a quiet affair with each of them seemingly lost in their own thoughts. When it was over, Ginny went back to the nursery to give Damon his final bottle of the evening, and Philip retreated behind the *Wall Street Journal*.

"Why has he not gone out yet?" Lydia worried out loud as she followed Ginny to the nursery.

"Don't worry," Ginny soothed. "It's early yet. Give him time."

But an hour later it was beginning to look as if time wasn't what Philip needed. A good shove was. He had finished the *Journal* and moved on to a Greek paper, totally oblivious to Lydia's increasing nervousness.

Finally he finished it and got to his feet. "I'll be in the study making a few phone calls," he said.

Lydia watched him go, a tragic expression on her face. "He is not going to go out this evening!"

"This is ridiculous! We are adult women, not children. We can go anywhere we please. We simply won't tell him where we're going," Ginny added at Lydia's uncertain expression.

"You mean lie?" Lydia asked.

"I wouldn't recommend it. It takes practice to be able to tell a believable lie. Our best bet is not to say anything. We'll leave while he's in the study."

"He will not like it," Lydia whispered with an uneasy glance at the closed study door.

"Probably not," Ginny conceded. "But look on the bright side. He can't do anything about it until we get back. And even then, all he can do is yell."

"I will do it." Lydia's face unexpectedly set in determined lines that for a second reminded Ginny of Philip. "Let us go now."

Ginny hurriedly grabbed up her purse, checked to make sure she had money and followed Lydia out through the kitchen entrance. Ginny didn't like sneaking out of the apartment like a Victorian parlor maid off to meet an admirer, but she couldn't see any practical alternative on such short notice. And there was nothing Philip could do about their flight, Ginny assured herself. Absolutely nothing.

Seven

"Quit looking over your shoulder," Ginny whispered to Lydia as they entered the art gallery. "People will think we're fugitives."

"That is the way I feel. I…" Lydia's face paled alarmingly as she stared over Ginny's left shoulder.

"What's wrong?" Ginny demanded.

Lydia swallowed, took a deep breath and swallowed again. "Act casually," she whispered frantically.

Ginny resisted the impulse to turn and check out the people behind her. "Your artist?"

Lydia nodded. Nervously, she brushed back a wisp of her black hair with fingers that shook. "Ginny! He is coming toward us."

"Good," Ginny said. "That's why we came. To see him."

"But I am not sure I want him to see me! He…"

"Lydia, it really is you," a male voice said.

Curious, Ginny turned. Immediately behind her was a slightly built man, at least an inch shorter than Lydia, with a wispy beard and hunched shoulders. *This* was Lydia's artist! Ginny stared at him in shock. If he wasn't the most unprepossessing specimen of masculinity she had ever seen, he had to be the second. Apparently love really was blind!

Ginny glanced from the uncertain smile on the man's thin face to Lydia's frozen expression.

Ginny silently counted to ten, and when neither of them said anything, she decided to help.

"I take it you are the creator of these?" Ginny tried.

Steward Morris gave her a blank look as if trying to figure out what she was talking about.

"I'm Ginny Alton. I came with Lydia."

Steward took the hand Ginny offered, holding it limply as if he weren't sure what he was supposed to do with it. Ginny tugged it free.

"Ginny is my brother's...friend," Lydia finally said. "She is very interested in art."

"I really like the way you've managed to capture the greenish tint of the sea in that picture." Ginny nodded toward the canvas beside them.

"He uses a black undercoat," Lydia announced with as much pride as if she'd painted it herself.

Steward smiled besottedly at Lydia. "You remembered what I told you that afternoon."

"Every word," Lydia assured him, and then blushed a brilliant red.

A flush that was echoed in Steward's thin cheeks. Ginny watched them, feeling ancient. Lydia might be older than she was and the mother of three children, but, emotionally, she didn't seem to have a clue.

"I'd very much like to show you some of my favorites,"
Steward told Lydia.

"Thank you." Lydia took his hand, and they moved
away as if they'd forgotten Ginny's existence.

Ginny watched them go, beginning to have doubts about
the wisdom of her having encouraged Lydia to come this
evening. She wasn't sure exactly what she'd expected to
happen when Lydia met her old flame, but she definitely
hadn't counted on their total preoccupation with each other.

"Lydia seems to be very well acquainted with Mr. Morris."

Ginny glanced up when she realized that the words were
aimed at her. She found a young woman dressed in the
height of fashion standing beside her.

"Steward Morris is just a friend." Ginny felt a shiver of
distaste at the woman's avid expression.

"But Lydia is a widow." The woman's voice sharpened.

Ginny raised her eyebrows. "You favor the old Indian
practice of a widow throwing herself on her husband's fu-
neral pyre?"

"Of course not, but—"

"Creon is dead and presumably enjoying himself in
heaven, so why shouldn't Lydia find what comfort she can
on earth?"

The woman blinked. "What an interesting viewpoint."

"Oh, I can't claim credit for it. It's a basic tenet of Chris-
tianity. Haven't you run across it before?" Ginny gave her
a bland smile.

The woman scowled and switched her line of interro-
gation. "Aren't you and Philip..." She allowed her voice
to trail away meaningfully.

"Aren't Philip and I what?" Ginny asked.

"You know." The woman leaned closer, and Ginny was
engulfed in a cloud of very expensive French perfume.

"I know lots of things." Ginny tried not to let her revulsion at the woman's single-minded quest for gossip
show. "And now if you'll excuse me, I want to look at
some of the things I don't know. Such as these paintings."

Ginny turned her back on the startled woman and walked
toward a collection of oils at the other end of the room.
She spent the next half hour studying Steward's paintings
and fending off people who seemed far more interested in
her sexual life than was polite. Even in the self-indulgent
world of the rich.

The only thing that kept Ginny from hiding in a stall in
the ladies' room was her desire to keep an eye on Lydia.
She felt responsible for her being here and, if something
should go wrong, Ginny wanted to be near enough to help.

Trouble, when it appeared, did not come from a source
that Ginny had anticipated. She had just escaped from a
dowager who was trying to grill her about how well Lydia
knew Steward Morris when a flurry of movement by the
entrance caught her attention and she glanced over. Pleasure scorched over her nerve endings and then just as
quickly ebbed, leaving her feeling light-headed.

Philip! Eagerly she studied the lean planes of his face,
lingering on his firm lips. Her own began to tingle at the
memory of kissing him. She wanted nothing so much as to
throw her arms around him and feel his body pressed
against hers. Ginny shook her head, trying to dislodge her
erotic fantasies.

This wasn't the time for self-indulgence. She could do
that later. Always provided that Philip was still talking to
her when he discovered what she'd done.

But maybe he wouldn't find out. Ginny quickly scanned
the crowd, looking for Lydia and her artist. She finally
found them half-hidden behind a marble column. All she
had to do was distract Philip long enough for Lydia to

realize that he was here. Once she knew, Lydia would want to leave and Philip would follow. With just a little bit of luck, he would never know who the featured artist at this show had been.

Ginny took a deep, steadying breath. As a plan of action it wasn't perfect, but it was the best she could do on the spur of the moment. She hurried across the room toward Philip.

Philip looked up from the woman who was holding on to his jacket sleeve as if she expected him to try to make a break for it, and his eyes narrowed as he caught sight of Ginny.

Ginny felt a curious sense of exultation fill her at his suddenly alert expression. She could hardly wait to begin to try to outwit him.

Stepping around the woman as if he'd forgotten she was there, Philip went to meet Ginny.

"What are you doing here?" he demanded.

"I don't know about you, but I generally go to art shows to look at the exhibits."

He looked around in disgust. "This isn't art."

"Shhh!" Taking his hand, Ginny urged him toward an abstract sculpture at the back of the room. She didn't know how much influence Philip had among these people, but Lydia would be very unhappy if Philip were to tarnish Steward's showing.

"Where are we going?" he asked.

"Somewhere where your rudeness can't be overheard!"

"Rudeness! We were invited to give our opinion."

"You were not invited. Lydia was. You gate-crashed. Why are you here?"

"Because I was worried about the pair of you! Do you have any idea of what can happen to two women out alone at night?"

Ginny grinned at him. "They get accosted by irrational men?"

"I am not irrational!"

"How did you find us anyway?" she asked curiously.

"It wasn't easy," he muttered, refusing to give her the satisfaction of knowing just how difficult it had been for him to first track down the taxi company that had picked her and Lydia up and then to find the individual driver who'd delivered them here. If the doorman at the apartment building hadn't noticed them leaving, he never would have been able to find them.

"Now that I've found you, would you mind telling me why you felt it necessary to sneak out of the apartment?"

"We didn't sneak," Ginny lied. "As adult women, we walked. And we came because we wanted to."

Philip looked around in disbelief. "You mean to tell me that you actually like this...stuff?"

"Some of it is quite...colorful."

"So's a train wreck!" he shot back. "But that doesn't make it a good idea."

"One should always keep an open mind," she countered, surreptitiously trying to discover whether or not Lydia was aware yet that Philip was here.

"If the artist's mind were any more open, it would have holes! Who did these?"

"I think someone said that he was local," Ginny said, tensing when she saw Lydia and Steward emerge from behind an exhibit about twenty feet from them.

"Come see one of my favorites." Ginny grabbed Philip's arm, momentarily losing her sense of urgency as her fingers closed around his muscular forearm. Valiantly she tried to ignore the feel of his muscles moving beneath the smooth material of his suit jacket as she tugged him in the opposite direction from Lydia.

"There." Ginny gestured toward a large canvas filled with pastel splotches. "It reminds me of springtime."

"It reminds me of man's gullibility."

Ginny looked down her nose at him. "Not being a man, I wouldn't know."

"I noticed that." Philip gave her a slow smile that sent her heartbeat rocketing. "In fact, I..."

Tension of a different kind gripped Ginny as she saw his eyes suddenly widen and a dark flush stain his cheekbones.

"What the hell!" He took a step toward Lydia and Steward.

Ginny clutched him, digging her fingers into his arm in warning. "Don't you dare!" she stressed. "Lydia will never forgive you if you cause a scene."

"And I'll never forgive myself if I allow that...that..."

"Friend of your sister's," Ginny supplied. "Behave yourself!"

"You don't understand," he muttered, although to Ginny's relief he didn't try to shake her off.

She had to get him out of here, Ginny decided. Away from Lydia and all the curious onlookers while he somehow calmed down. Tucking his hand into the crook of her arm, she headed toward the back of the room, to the hall leading to the rest rooms. To her relief, he went with her.

"Where are we going?" he demanded.

"Someplace private where you can cool off." She opened the first door past the rest rooms, looking for an empty room. What she found was an oversize closet filled with what looked like cleaning supplies.

Ginny was about to close the door when she heard the sound of high heels clicking on the marble flooring. Hurriedly she shoved Philip into the closet and scrambled in after him. She quietly pulled the door shut and listened as the footsteps passed and finally disappeared into the ladies' room.

She didn't want Philip to talk to anyone in his present mood. As mad as he was and as deeply into gossip as some of these women were, who knew what might happen.

"Tell me, has it generally been your experience that people cool off best when forced into closets?" Philip asked.

"Hush," she muttered as she heard another set of footsteps go past.

"That's not the way to get me to be quiet," he murmured.

Ginny felt a prickle of excitement as Philip's breath warmed the back of her neck. She turned to find him just inches from her. Heat, scented by the faintly tangy cologne he favored, was radiated from his body.

A flood of desire engulfed her, submerging her reason for being here in the first place. Somehow, Lydia and Steward no longer seemed as important as they had. Her entire world had narrowed to the man standing inches from her.

Ginny stared up through the dim light into his eyes. They seemed to glow with the strength of his feelings. For her. Anticipation rolled through her, luring her even closer to him.

Reaching out, Ginny ran her fingertip over his jawline. His reaction was instantaneous. Grabbing her, he pulled her up against him. Her body arched into his and a small yearning sound escaped her as her breasts seemed to swell, absorbing the heat of his body and using it to feed her own passions.

Philip grasped her chin and tilted her face up. His mouth closed over hers with an intense longing he made no effort to disguise. Exerting pressure, he molded the contours of her mouth to his and teased them apart.

Ginny eagerly opened her lips, welcoming his tongue's

invasion. He tasted of brandy and coffee and vibrant masculinity as his tongue engaged hers in a sensual duel.

A shivery desire began to grow in her, pushing rational thought to the very edge of her consciousness. The need to feel his bare skin against hers was fast becoming an overwhelming compulsion. Ginny began to tremble as the heavy throbbing sensation in her abdomen intensified, making her feel slightly frantic. Her only reality was Philip and her need for him. She wanted him in the most basic way possible, and the only thing that was going to stop her from having him was Philip himself.

Speculatively, Ginny stared up at him through slitted eyelids. His face was set in rigid lines that told her far more clearly than words just how aroused he was. Inching back slightly, she shoved his tie over his shoulder and fumbled with the buttons on his shirt. She needed to feel him. To caress his bare skin. She had to find an outlet for the desire rampaging through her before she burst with the effort it was taking to contain it.

Ginny finally managed to get his shirt open enough to expose his chest. Placing her hands flat against his rib cage, Ginny pushed upward. His chest hair scraped abrasively over her palms, sending pleasure ricocheting over her nerves. The sensation tightened the need building up in her to almost unbearable levels. She couldn't wait any longer. Ginny groped for his belt buckle.

Impatiently pushing her fingers out of the way, Philip yanked his belt open and ripped down his pants zipper.

Eagerly Ginny tugged the swollen length of him free from his clothes. Satisfaction at the feel of his heat against her fingers provided a momentary respite for her driving sense of urgency. He was so quintessentially male. And at the moment he was all hers.

"I want you." Philip's voice was hoarse and his movements jerky, not at all like his usual fluid grace.

Lowering his head, he captured her mouth with a raw desire that Ginny found an incredible aphrodisiac. His hot tongue shoved inside her mouth, and Ginny whimpered longingly as he moved in a sensual parody of the greater intimacy.

His large hands cupped her hips, and he lifted her slightly, cradling her against his hard body. Ginny pressed against his throbbing manhood, and the action sent heated sparks of desire racing over her nerves.

"We need…" he muttered distractedly, but she barely heard him. She already knew what she needed. Him. What he didn't know was how to go about getting him in their present circumstances.

Philip apparently had some ideas of his own. Pulling up her full skirt, he grasped her panty hose and pulled them down over her hips.

"Yes," Ginny muttered encouragingly as he cupped the hot moist center of her feelings. "Ah, it…" Her voice became suspended as he rubbed lightly over the tiny center of her desire and a violent shudder twisted through her.

Bracing his back against the wall, Philip spread his legs and, digging his fingers into her bare hips, he lifted her up.

Ginny instinctively grasped his broad shoulders, hanging on as she felt the hot length of him probing at her core. An explosive gasp escaped her as he suddenly drove into her. Instinctively she wrapped her legs around his waist and clung to the whole delicious length of him. He felt so fantastic. So… Her thoughts began to blur as he used his hands to force her back and forth against his heated length. Emotion spiraled through her building to a clamorous pitch. It was as if the very unconventionality of their surroundings

had telescoped her feelings. Distilling them to their mos
primitive state.

Ginny arched her head back as her feelings finally buil
to the point where she could no longer contain them, an
she shuddered violently, clenching her teeth to hold back
the sounds of pleasure bubbling out of her throat. Her self
absorption was so great that she barely noticed when Philip
suddenly went rigid and then erupted in a sensual firestorm
of feeling. The only thing that concerned her at the momen
was her own feelings of satisfaction.

It was the sound of a man's heavy tread in the hallway
outside that finally penetrated the sensual fog that gripped
Ginny, and she muttered protests against Philip's damp
neck. She didn't want to return to the everyday world. She
wanted to stay right where she was. Adrift with Philip on
a sea of sensuality.

Languidly she touched the tip of her tongue against his
salty skin, smiling in satisfaction as he jerked convulsively.
Even now, wrapped in his arms, she found it hard to believe
that she could have such a powerful effect on such a sophisticated man that he was willing to make love to her in
a broom closet.

And if the role of impetuous lover seemed an unlikely
one for Philip, then herself in the role of femme fatale was
totally unbelievable. She'd always been so conventional before. And yet there was nothing the least bit conventional—
or rational—about her reaction to Philip. In Philip's arms
she had discovered an emotional depth that seemed limit-
less.

Philip dropped a quick kiss on her forehead and murmured, "We should get out of here before anyone finds
us."

Ginny stiffened her languid muscles and forced herself
to move away from him. "I can see the headlines now."

he tried for a light tone as she straightened her clothing. "Tycoon Caught In Love Tryst Among The Brooms."

Philip grinned at her. "Is that what we were doing? Trysting? I've always wondered what that meant."

"Well, wonder no more. You are a full-fledged tryster."

As well as a very confused man, Philip thought uneasily as he rebuttoned the shirt he couldn't remember unbuttoning. If someone had ever told him that he'd make love to a woman in a broom closet at an art show he'd have told them they were out of their minds, and yet... All he had to do was to look at Ginny, and he seemed to act entirely out of character.

Was that what had happened to Creon? The poisonous thought suddenly punctured his sense of pleasure. Had Creon taken one look at Ginny and forgotten Lydia?

Lydia! Philip tensed as he suddenly remembered why Ginny had hustled him into the closet in the first place. Lydia was out there with Steward Morris. How could he have forgotten?

"What's the matter?" Ginny noticed his sudden rigidity.

"I just remembered that Lydia is out there doing who knows what with that damn artist."

"People who live in glass houses shouldn't throw stones."

Philip frowned at her. "What does that mean, and why are you scrambling around on the floor?"

"I'm trying to find my other shoe, and as for what it means, think about it, my fellow tryster."

Philip grabbed her arm and pulled her upward to face him.

"Are you telling me that my sister is...is having sex with that..."

Pain ripped through Ginny at his outraged expression. He obviously thought there was nothing wrong with his

having an affair with her, but the thought of his sister doing
the same was unthinkable.

"I'm not telling you anything of the sort," Ginny bit
out. "I wouldn't presume to question your sister about her
sex life. It's none of my business. Or yours!" Finally locating her missing shoe, she jammed her foot into it.

Ignoring Philip's rasped command to wait, Ginny flung
open the closet door and stalked out into the hallway. It
was empty, but at the moment she didn't care who knew
what she'd been doing. She was too full of anguish to
worry about something as insignificant as embarrassment.

"Ginny!" Philip caught up with her at the end of the
deserted hallway. "What's wrong?"

"You want the short list or the long list?" she snapped.

"Philip! There you are! Emily thought she saw you earlier, and then we couldn't find you." A portly middle-aged
man hurried up to them.

"Excuse me." Ginny gave the frustrated Philip a patiently fake smile and escaped. She needed to be alone for
a moment while she tried to get her chaotic emotions under
some sort of control.

Slipping into a deserted alcove hung with small oils of
various wildflowers, Ginny stared at a white-and-pink
flower and ran through her stress-reduction routine. It
helped. Not as much as it usually did, but enough that she
could think about her reaction with something approaching
her normal logic.

Philip's double standard hurt, she conceded, but mad-
dening as it was, she still wasn't exactly sure why it bothered her so much. She certainly didn't want the restricted
kind of life Lydia led. She liked being able to make her
own decisions.

Ginny sighed. And now she was stuck with the consequences of one of those decisions. So what did she want

o do about it? She chewed her lower lip uncertainly. Blaming Philip was hardly fair even if it was more satisfying than blaming herself.

He hadn't lied to her. She hadn't even lied to herself. She'd known of his antiquated viewpoint. She simply hadn't cared at the time. And she had the disheartening feeling that if Philip were to take her in his arms, she wouldn't care again. At least, not until he stopped kissing her.

Which left her with two choices. She could continue down the path she'd chosen and allow herself to make love to Philip every chance she got, or she could withdraw in offended silence and refuse to have anything more to do with him.

A sharp feeling of panic wrapped itself around her chest, interfering with her breathing. She didn't want to push him away. Not until she absolutely had to. And sooner or later she would. She knew it. Philip and she came from different worlds and, while she had no trouble fitting into his bed, fitting into his world was another matter entirely. Women in Philip's world were supposed to be like Lydia, quietly subservient to the men in their families. They spent their time in a mind-deadening round of social events that seemed entirely pointless to Ginny. A career to them meant a husband and children. Certainly not work outside the home. Ginny knew such a narrow life would drive her to distraction in a very short time.

She sighed, knowing that her heart had already made its decision. For better or worse, she wanted whatever Philip was willing to share with her for as long as he would.

Straightening her shoulders, Ginny went looking for Lydia. She found her standing with Philip, Steward and a man that Ginny vaguely remembered as being the gallery owner. It was not a comfortable-looking group. Philip

looked coldly furious; Lydia looked about to cry; Steward
looked scared, but determined; and the gallery owner
looked confused.

Stand up to Philip, Ginny mentally urged Lydia as she
hurried over to them.

Lydia didn't. She simply stood there, growing paler and
paler and twisting her hands together ineffectively.

"I have a headache, Lydia. Would you mind terribly if
we were to go home now?" Ginny said as she reached
them, deciding that the best thing to do would be to get
Lydia away before she burst into tears and provided more
grist for the gossip mill.

"Yes, of course we can go home," Lydia eagerly agreed.

"I very much enjoyed your work, Steward, particularly
the sea scenes." Ginny tried to put a semblance of nor-
malcy on their departure. "I hope to come back before I
leave for home, and pick out one of them."

"I will come and help you decide," Lydia said with a
nervous glance at Philip.

"Goodbye, Steward," Lydia said as Philip hustled her
toward the door.

"Goodbye." Ginny nodded at the gallery owner and hurried after them.

"You must be rich beyond the dreams of avarice, Philip
Lysander." Ginny launched an offensive once they were in
his car.

"Why do you say that?" Lydia asked when Philip didn't
reply.

"Because only money would make people ignore his
appalling behavior," Ginny said. "He better hope he never
loses it, or he'll never get invited anywhere."

"Quit trying to change the subject," Philip bit out.

"Since no one was saying anything when I spoke, I in-
troduced a subject—I didn't change it," Ginny retorted.

Philip audibly ground his teeth, while Lydia scrunched
down further into the soft leather car seat.

"Lydia, you are not to see that...that..." Philip sputtered.

"Has he always had this problem with names?" Ginny
asked Lydia with mock concern. "He can't remember Damon's and, now he can't seem to remember Steward's."

"He's usually good with names," Lydia mumbled.

"Then maybe he's just getting old and his memory's
ailing." Ginny gave him a commiserating smile.

"I am not getting old!" Philip yelled and then flushed
when the driver in the lane beside him suddenly slammed
on his brakes and gave Philip a startled look. "And you
will stay out of this."

"No," Ginny said succinctly. "Lydia is my friend."

Lydia gave Ginny a look of such abject gratitude that
Ginny felt like crying. Poor Lydia. She might have money
and social position, but she didn't have much real happiness
in her life.

"And she's my sister, and I say that she's not to see that
gigolo again."

"Gigolo!" Ginny hooted. "They don't have gigolos
anymore, and even when they did, they were smooth, sophisticated men. More like you than Steward Morris. No, I
take that back," Ginny tried to cover her inadvertent slip.
"Gigolos tried to make themselves agreeable to women.
You couldn't make yourself agreeable if your life depended
on it. Why shouldn't Lydia see her friend if she wants to?"

"She's a widow!" Philip snapped.

"Strange how many Greeks seem to think that life stops
at widowhood," Ginny said tartly.

"Later it would be all right," Philip insisted. "But it's
too soon after Creon's death."

"I can't remember if it was Abby Van Buren or Ann

Landers who said that it wasn't what you do after your spouse is dead that counts, it's how you treated them when they were alive, but whichever it was, they were right.' Ginny gave Philip a long, level look.

It sent a chill of apprehension through him. Surely she wasn't insinuating that she'd tell Lydia about Creon's infidelity, was she?

Philip pressed his lips together in frustration. Ginny would, he admitted to himself. She'd do it under the mistaken impression that she was helping Lydia. But Lydia wasn't like Ginny. Ginny was strong. She practically radiated self-confidence, while even before Creon's death Lydia had had to be constantly shielded from life's misfortunes.

Once they got back to the apartment, he'd talk to Ginny. She meant well, but she simply didn't understand. He'd make her understand just how fragile Lydia's nerves had always been. How she needed to be shielded from men like that fortune hunter, Steward Morris.

His fingers instinctively tightened on the steering wheel as he remembered their fantastic interlude in the broom closet. He still didn't understand exactly what had happened. All he'd meant to do was to kiss her, but somehow when he'd touched her... Desire welled through him, and all he could think about was making love to her again. This time slowly and leisurely.

Later, he promised himself. First he'd make her understand about Lydia, and then once he'd cleared the air, he'd take her in his arms.... The car suddenly shot forward as his desire to get home became a burning need.

Eight

Ginny tucked a thin cotton blanket around Damon and, bending over the crib, gave him a kiss. Damon didn't stir and, satisfied that he was settled for the night, she whispered a good-night to Nanny who was reading a horror story.

Nanny gave her an absent smile and went back to her book.

Ginny grimaced as she left the nursery. Nothing was as clear-cut to her as it had seemed when she'd first arrived in Greece. Philip was far more than just the arrogant, male chauvinist she'd first thought, Lydia was more than just Creon's wronged wife, and sweet, gentle Nanny was a devotee of Stephen King.

Almost nothing, Ginny amended as she crossed the apartment's empty living room. Jason Papas hadn't changed. He was still a willfully blind, egocentric fool who seemed to live his life on some version of the divine right of kings.

And the longer she was around the man, the less sure she was of the wisdom of Beth's desire that he recognize Damon as his grandson.

Beth wouldn't have a clue as to how to cope with Jason and, if he did recognize Damon, would he also think that his money entitled him to run the baby's life?

Ginny chewed her lower lip worriedly. If only she could find some way to have a long, uninterrupted conversation with Beth, instead of these hastily snatched reports she had to make.

Ginny rubbed her forehead, which was beginning to ache slightly. Stress, she accurately diagnosed her problem as she opened the door to her bedroom.

"Is the boy settled for the night?"

Ginny jumped at the unexpected sound of Philip's deep voice. She jerked around to find him sitting on the chaise longue by the window, and a frisson of pleasure nudged aside the pain of her headache. She knew that it was probably better for her stress levels if Philip hadn't come into her bedroom, but she had the rest of her life to work on her peace of mind and only a few days more to enjoy Philip's company. A sliver of pain dented her happiness as she remembered just how short her remaining time with him really was. Determinedly she shook off the morose feeling.

"Damon, also known as 'the boy,' is sleeping."

"Good." He ignored her sarcasm. "I need to talk to you about tonight."

Ginny felt her headache intensify at his implacable expression. She didn't want another postmortem on how she wasn't supposed to read anything into his lovemaking. Nor did she feel up to dealing with his attempts to protect his sister. Just once it would be nice if he protected her from unpleasantness.

"You don't *need* to talk to me," Ginny contradicted him.

"You might chose to do so, but you certainly don't need to."

Philip frowned, his dark brows almost meeting above his nose.

"You can divert a conversation quicker than anyone I've ever met," he complained.

Ginny perched on the end of the chaise longue, her attention caught by his long leg. The thin gray material of his suit pants was stretched tautly over his muscular thigh, and Ginny swallowed as she remembered the feel of his hair-roughened flesh against her own much softer thighs. The urge to touch him was growing, and she couldn't think of one good reason to deny herself the pleasure.

Slipping her hand under his pant leg, she rubbed her fingertips up over his silky sock.

Philip jerked and hastily moved his leg off the chaise longue. "You are not to encourage Lydia in this foolishness," he said.

Ginny gave him an impossibly innocent smile. "Oh? What foolishness is that?"

Philip scowled at her. "Don't play dumb with me. I know better."

"Really?" Ginny grinned at him as a feeling of exhilaration washed through her. She argued a lot with Philip, she suddenly realized, but she didn't find it threatening. Their arguments were more like mental jousting. With two equally matched opponents looking for an advantage. And they were equally matched, she conceded. Whether Philip was willing to admit it or not.

"I won't have her seeing that…" he sputtered to an inarticulate stop.

"Steward Morris," she supplied with pseudohelpfulness. "I swear I'm going to have placards made for you with people's names on them since you can't seem to keep them straight.''

"I don't want—''

"What you want isn't the question here,'' Ginny cut him off. ''It's what Lydia wants that's relevant.''

"She doesn't understand.''

Ginny sniffed. ''It seems to be a family failing. Tell me, Philip, what do you think Steward could possibly do to her that Creon hasn't already done?''

"I don't know that Creon is the boy's father.'' Philip didn't want to talk about Creon and his relationship with Ginny. He didn't even want to think about it. It made him feel murderous.

"All right, forget Creon for a moment,'' Ginny said. "Tell me what there is about Steward Morris that anyone could possibly find offensive.''

Philip stared at her in frustration. Why wouldn't she just once do as he told her to, instead of always arguing? Why was she always questioning the rules that he'd lived with all his life?

"They come from different worlds.'' He took refuge in one of his father's bromides.

Ginny hunched her shoulders against the sudden despairing weight that pressed down on her as she realized that that description applied to her as well as to Steward Morris.

"You have the makings of a first-class snob.'' Ginny tried to make Philip think about what he was saying. Not for her own sake, she rationalized, but for Lydia's.

"I am not a snob! I am a realist.''

"A rose by any other name,'' she shot back.

Philip ground his teeth. Why couldn't Ginny understand that he was worried about his sister? That Lydia was his responsibility. He'd promised his father that he'd take care of his sisters. It was his duty as head of the family to see that she was happy.

Had Lydia been happy with Creon? The sudden thought caught him off guard. Could she have known that Creon had been seeing Ginny when he'd been in New York? For that matter, was Ginny the only woman Creon had had an affair with? Creon had traveled extensively in his business. Could he have indulged in other affairs with other women in other cities?

An appalling image of a series of young women pounding on Jason's door and demanding that he provide for their children drifted through his mind. It wasn't something he wanted to think about. In fact, he didn't really want to talk about Lydia. Or about anything else for that matter. What he wanted to do was to make love to Ginny. To take her in his arms and slowly, leisurely make love to her all night long. That interlude in the closet had been wildly exciting, but it had been rather like gulping a fine old Napoleon brandy. You missed the best part if you didn't savor it. And he wanted to savor Ginny.

Philip studied Ginny uncertainly. But would she let him? She seemed to be in a strange mood. The only way to find out was to try, and he finally decided to chance it.

Slowly leaning toward her, he grasped her upper arms. When she didn't protest, he gently tugged her toward him. An immense feeling of anticipation filled him as he stared down into her beautiful face.

He ran his fingertips over the side of her cheek, relishing the texture of her skin. She felt like flower petals, velvety and incredibly delicate. His fingers wandered over her ear, learning each individual whirl. He could feel his body hardening, becoming swollen with longing and his thoughts blurring. As if his consciousness were being stretched to the breaking point by what he was feeling.

His arms tightened and he molded her pliant body more firmly against his. Her breasts pushed into his chest, urging him on. It was all he could do not to pounce on her like some adolescent who'd never learned self-control. But that was the way she made him feel, he realized. Like an adolescent who had just discovered sex. He didn't know why this woman, out of all the ones he'd known, affected him like that. He didn't even really care all that much. He was too busy enjoying it.

Philip studied her face intently, trying to decide where to start kissing her. The slight flicker of movement of her eyelashes caught his attention, and he brushed his lips across them. His arms tightened in response to the tremor he felt shake her slender body. She was so fantastically responsive to him. As if she were somehow attuned to his every need. He found the thought incredibly erotic.

The intrusive ringing of the telephone startled him out of his self-absorption. Much as he wanted to ignore it, he knew it wouldn't do any good. If he didn't answer it, Lydia would and, if it was the call from his investment manager he'd been expecting, then she'd come looking for him.

Raising his head, he stared down into Ginny's flushed face. He most emphatically didn't want company. Not even his sister's.

Steeling himself, he got to his feet.

Ginny shook her head, trying to dispel the disorientation that always seemed to cloud her mind when Philip touched her. She scrambled upright and watched as Philip picked up the phone on the bedside table. From the expression on his face, whatever was being said wasn't something Philip wanted to hear. He responded in a spate of clipped Greek and then abruptly hung up.

"Problems?" she asked, wanting to erase his frown.

"Just business," he muttered distractedly. "You

wouldn't understand." But even knowing that she wouldn't, he found that he still wanted to tell her. To share one of his growing number of problems with her. "Try me," Ginny said.

Philip shrugged. It wouldn't hurt to tell her, and verbalizing it might help to clarify it in his own mind. "That was Harry who heads up my company's overseas investments division. I own a substantial amount of stock in a Mexican firm called Mira Loma, which has been doing very poorly lately. Harry called to tell me that the man who founded the company was just ousted in a takeover bid by his brother. Harry feels that I should sell. That the company's performance will only get worse because the brother is a university professor, not a businessman."

"True, but Alfonso Hernandez's field is economics, and he's good enough at it to have been nominated for a Nobel Prize. Even more relevant to the company's future earnings is that Hernandez is actually the head of a consortium that includes an American of Mexican descent who has twenty years of successful experience running branches of American businesses in Juárez. Added to which, Hernandez has managed to convince a New York bank to make the company a sizable loan at a reasonable rate of interest in order to modernize the plant, and the union has agreed not to push for any concessions while Hernandez is trying to get the company back on its feet. And last, but not least, Hernandez has the inside track on a big contract to supply component parts for the Ford plant in Juárez."

Philip stared at her in shock. How could she know all that? Harry hadn't mentioned any of it.

"Who told you that?" Philip demanded.

Ginny looked down her nose at him, annoyed at his incredulous tone. "I got a news flash for you, friend. Modern women don't wait for anyone to tell them anything. They find out for themselves.''

"But..." Philip gestured ineffectively. "Why didn't Harry know all that?"

"He's not very good?"

"He should be better than a schoolteacher," Philip muttered, having the strong feeling that he was missing something, but unable to figure out what. How could a kindergarten teacher be so knowledgeable about the Mexican economy?

That was a mistake, Ginny admonished herself. She should have remembered that Beth wouldn't have known that. She most definitely didn't want him to start wondering about her background. With his resources he might find out the truth, and then her short time with him would be over. And the best way to stop him from thinking was to indulge in what she really wanted to do anyway. Make love to him.

Getting to her feet, she walked toward him. She'd never intentionally tried to seduce anyone in her life, let alone a sophisticated man like Philip. But she intended to give it a try.

Ginny stopped inches from him and gave him what she hoped was a sultry look. Reaching out, she ran her palm down over his cheek. A burst of excitement tore through her as she felt the tension in his muscles. Philip was nowhere near as calm as he appeared. The thought exhilarated her. With any luck at all, in five minutes he wouldn't remember his own name let alone some Mexican company's.

Ginny inched closer, until her breasts were brushing against the front of his shirt. A tremor shot through her as her nipples convulsed. Her breasts felt heavy and tingly. Her eyelids drooped as her vision centered inward, concentrating on what she was feeling.

Ginny moved sensuously against him, and the resulting

cascade of feeling threatened to overwhelm her. She wanted to make love to him so much. Wanted to feel his heavy weight pressing her down into the bed. Wanted to feel him moving within her.

She fumbled with the buttons on his shirt with fingers that felt clumsy and awkward. As if her mind were too busy feeling to bother to send coherent instructions to her fingers.

Finally freeing the buttons, Ginny pushed open his shirt and pressed her face against his chest. She took a deep breath. He smelled delicious. A blend of scents that was uniquely Philip. Ginny rubbed her cheek over his chest, shivering as his crisp hair rasped over her tender skin.

"You smell so wonderful," she muttered, "but you have too many clothes on."

A satisfied smile curved her lips as she felt his heartbeat suddenly skyrocket. His obvious fascination with her was almost as big a turn-on as his effect on her. But not quite.

Philip nuzzled the soft skin on her cheekbone and his hot breath stirred her hair, making her shiver.

"Let's trade," he murmured.

Ginny licked her dry lips, mentally scrambling to make sense of his words. "Trade what?"

"Clothes." His voice sounded deepened perceptibly. "One for one."

A shivery sensation composed of equal parts desire and anticipation shot through her, raising goose bumps as it went.

Quickly matching his words to action, Philip shrugged out of his shirt and let it fall. "Your turn."

Ginny looked at the gleaming white shirt lying on the pale blue carpeting and felt her stomach twist in excitement. This game had distinct possibilities.

Taking a deep steadying breath, she unzipped her dress

and allowed it to drop to the floor. Stepping out of it, she peered up at him expectantly.

"You are so beautiful," Philip murmured. "The most beautiful woman I've ever seen."

Ginny shivered at his sensuous tone. He made her feel like a combination of Cleopatra and Marilyn Monroe. It was an intoxicating feeling that made her feel capable of almost anything.

Her breath caught in her throat as Philip unzipped his pants and kicked them off, along with his shoes. A suffocating feeling engulfed her at the sight of his swollen manhood pressing against his white briefs.

"Your turn," he whispered, and in a daze Ginny unfastened her bra and let it fall.

She tensed in anticipation as Philip reached out and cupped her right breast in his hand. A tingling sensation sizzled over her skin at his light touch. Instinctively Ginny pushed forward, intensifying the pressure of his rough palm against her sensitive skin. She could feel her nipple hardening, and an aching feeling began to throb deep in her abdomen.

She wanted to make love to him now. Right this minute. She wanted to skip the appetizers and go right to the main course. Stepping back, she hastily shrugged out of her panty hose and the tiny silk panties she was wearing, then pointedly stared at his briefs.

"Oh, yes," he muttered. "Definitely." In one quick movement, he was gloriously nude.

Ginny barely had time to enjoy the sight when he suddenly scooped her up in his arms.

Grasping his shoulders to balance herself, she asked, "What are you doing?"

"I always wanted to grab a beautiful, naked woman and

carry her off somewhere,'' he confided. ''And they don't
come any more beautiful or nakeder than you are.''

''Really?'' Ginny nuzzled the hollow at the base of his
neck and then licked it. A tremor shot through him which
fired her own sense of excitement.

''Really.'' He chuckled and the sound was slightly ragged. ''It's one of many fantasies that I've entertained over
the years.''

Ginny lightly nibbled on his earlobe, relishing the salty
taste of his skin. ''You must show me a few others.''

''Sometime.'' He carefully set her down in the middle
of the bed and then dropped down beside her. ''The problem with acting out fantasies is it takes a lot of control.''

''Oh?'' Ginny lightly ran her fingertips over his chest,
pausing to lightly flick his flat nipples with her fingernail.
A smile teased her lips when Philip shuddered.

''The problem is that I don't seem to be able to muster
much control when I'm making love to you.''

His words echoed meaninglessly in Ginny's ears. She
was too busy trying to get a handle on her own reactions
as Philip slowly, tantalizingly lowered himself onto her. His
heavy weight pressed her down, holding her captive. It was
a fantastically erotic sensation, and Ginny wiggled slightly,
unable to remain still. She could feel his manhood burning
against her abdomen, but fantastic as the feeling was, it
wasn't enough. Not nearly enough. She wanted him deep
inside her. She wanted to absorb him into her very being.
She wanted...

A sound of shocked pleasure whistled out of her lungs
as he lifted himself slightly and probed the moistness between her legs with his finger. A yearning whimper of desire escaped her as she lifted her hips against his hand. She
felt burning hot, as if the top layer of her skin were on fire.
The feeling intensified significantly when Philip grasped

her turgid nipple and gently tugged on it. Sensation swept
through her, building to an urgency that defied rational
thought. An urgency that Philip clearly shared.

Carefully positioning himself, he thrust forward in a
slow, steady motion.

"Philip!" Ginny gasped as the hard, hot length of him
filled her. Clutching his shoulders, she pulled him close as
she wrapped her legs around his lean waist, trying to force
him even deeper. He felt so...

Her mind blurred as he captured her mouth and roughly
shoved his tongue inside. Ginny trembled violently, having
trouble containing the emotions churning through her. She
didn't know how much more of this she could stand before
she went stark raving mad.

Philip began to rock back and forth with slow, deliberate
movements, drawing her deeper and deeper into the seething whirlpool of sensation he was creating. Excitement
wound itself tighter and tighter around her stunned mind
until at last she couldn't contain it any longer. It began to
spill out of her, finally exploding into a paroxysm of pleasure so intense, she didn't think she'd survive. Ginny barely
even noticed when Philip found his own pleasure and collapsed on her.

It was the frantic beating of his heart pounding against
her breasts that finally penetrated Ginny's intense self-
absorption, allowing her to slowly surface through the
clouds of sexual pleasure fogging her mind. A satisfied
smile curved her lips at the way Philip was limply sprawled
across her. Somehow it intensified her own pleasure to
know that he'd shared her reactions. Gently she ran her
finger down over the slight bump of his spine. He jerked
and her arms possessively closed around him. She didn't
want him to move. She wanted him right where he was.

Still inside her. That way, when he recovered a bit, he might make love to her all over again.

Ginny trembled longingly as she felt him begin to grow hard again. It was going to be a wonderful night, she thought dreamily. A wonderful night followed by a wonderful day.

She was right about the night. It fulfilled her every expectation. It was the following day that proved a disappointment. Philip had come to the breakfast table in a preoccupied mood. A mood that took a distinct turn for the worse when he received an early phone call.

"Yes, yes, no!" he bit out and then replaced the receiver with a decided snap.

Ginny looked up at his curt tone. A tremor of unease shot through her as she wondered who he'd been talking to. Jason, possibly? Could it be something about Damon? Or about her and Beth?

"A problem?" Ginny asked cautiously.

Philip snorted. "If stupidity can be thought to be a problem, but the way the world operates these days, it seems to be the norm."

"What can not be cured must be endured." Lydia added another spoonful of sugar to her coffee.

"Maybe," Ginny said doubtfully, "but first I'd want to make sure that I couldn't cure a problem before I took the long-suffering approach."

"I'll cure it all right." Philip shoved his fingers through his hair in frustration. "If I have to smack a few heads together to do it. This whole thing is nothing more than a few local union officials trying to build their own power base at the company's expense. And while all I stand to lose is a little money, the workers could lose their jobs.

There are too many manufacturers only too eager to grab our contracts if we default.''

He turned to his sister. "Lydia, if Jason calls, tell him I've gone to the factory.''

Ginny bit her lip to hold back her disappointed protest. She didn't want Philip to go anywhere. She wanted him to stay right where he was. Here in the apartment with her. Even if he spent the whole day closeted in his study, at least he would be here. And there was always the possibility that he might take a break.

She swallowed as her stomach contracted with longing as ideas of how they might spend his breaks drifted through her mind. It wasn't fair, Ginny thought unhappily as Philip tossed an absent goodbye at her and left. She had so little time to be with Philip. Soon she'd have to go back to New York. Not only did Beth need her, but she couldn't stay away from her office indefinitely. To lose what little time she did have to a bunch of fools who couldn't or wouldn't make an effort to understand the economic realities of the modern world was intolerable. And asking Philip to ignore the strike was no good. She knew him well enough to know that he'd never shirk what he felt to be his duty. Certainly not just to please her. Ginny stifled a sigh as she heard the front door slam behind Philip.

Listlessly she got to her feet, no longer interested in food, and went to see what Damon was doing. Maybe she and Lydia could go sightseeing while the babies took their naps this afternoon. She tried to work up some enthusiasm for the idea. And she could find a public phone and call Beth.

Lydia was totally uninterested in venturing out into the heat and humidity of Athens, so Ginny went by herself and then wished she hadn't bothered. Not only had Beth not been home, but Ginny couldn't muster more than a tepid interest in the wonders of the ancient world. Her emotions were too firmly centered on the wonders of Philip's love-making.

She missed Philip's presence, Ginny admitted. Without him there, it seemed as if a vital component was lacking from her life. As if reality had somehow been watered down. It was a sobering realization, and one that she would have preferred not to have made. Especially considering the fact that very shortly she was going to have to learn to get along without ever seeing Philip again.

A chill of foreboding tightened her skin. She knew their relationship wouldn't work long-term. And the major reason it wouldn't work was because Philip didn't want it to. Ginny squarely faced the fact. To Philip she could never be more than a momentary distraction. His rigid upbringing had seen to that. Ginny swallowed against an uncharacteristic urge to burst into self-pitying tears.

Finally giving up on sight-seeing, Ginny took a cab back to the apartment, hoping that Philip might have returned. To her disappointment, not only wasn't Philip there, but Jason Papas was.

"Where have you been?" Jason yelled at Ginny the second she walked into the apartment.

"Out," Ginny replied, and forced a smile at the unhappy-looking Lydia. As well she might be, Ginny thought in sympathy, if she had been trying to entertain Jason when he was in this mood.

"I drove all the way into Athens to talk to you, and you weren't here!" Jason's thick gray eyebrows quivered angrily.

"I'd say that pretty much describes the situation," Ginny said. "And now if you'll excuse me, you'll have to wait a little longer. I want to check on Damon."

"I just did," Jason snapped. "He's asleep. We'll talk in Philip's study." He turned and stalked away.

Ginny looked at Lydia, who shrugged as if disclaiming all knowledge of the reason for Jason's temper.

Ginny followed Jason reluctantly. Much as she didn't want to talk to him, that was why she had come to Greece in the first place, she reminded herself.

Closing the study door behind her, Ginny looked at the old man. The muscles in his throat were moving as if he were trying to swallow something that didn't want to go down.

"The lab called this morning," Jason finally said.

Ginny merely waited for him to continue, assuming he was talking about a follow-up test he'd had done concerning his heart attack.

Jason's lips twisted bitterly. "They said there can be very little doubt that Damon really is my grandson. They compared the boy's blood with mine and found too many similarities in the DNA for him to be anything but a very close relative, and since the only way that could happen—"

"You took a blood sample from Damon without my consent?" Ginny demanded incredulously.

"How else was I supposed to get one? And, anyway, you should be happy. I'm willing to admit that the boy is my grandson." He glared at her. "I don't know how you managed to seduce Creon, but women like you know all the tricks."

Ginny made a monumental effort to swallow the fury bubbling through her at Jason's high-handedness. He had had absolutely no right to stick a needle in Damon. But he'd already done it. She tried to think rationally and not emotionally. It was over. Nothing she could do or say would change what had already happened.

Ginny stared into Jason's petulant face. And nothing she could say would ever change Jason Papas's mind. As far as he was concerned, Creon was nothing more than an innocent victim of Beth's devious feminine wiles.

Ginny took a deep breath and then another as she struggled to keep focused on Beth's needs and not on her own anger. Beth wanted Jason to acknowledge Damon. It was important to her. Ginny's personal feelings about the man were irrelevant.

"I discussed this with Philip," Jason continued, "and he agrees that Damon should remain here in Greece with me."

A crushing sense of betrayal squeezed through Ginny, leaving her light-headed. Philip actually was a party to trying to take Damon away from her? The fact that she wasn't really Damon's mother was irrelevant. Philip thought she was. He knew she loved Damon, and yet he still was willing to lend himself to a plan to turn a defenseless child over to Jason Papas.

Was that why Philip had made love to her? All her earlier doubts about his motives came surging back. To make her more amenable to the idea of giving Damon to Jason? Suffocating pain wrapped itself around her, making it hard for her to breathe and even harder to think clearly. Or was Philip's plan more sinister than that? Had he instigated an affair with her in order to try to discredit her in the eyes of a court if it should come to a custody battle?

If he had, he was in for a shock when he found out that Damon was her cousin's child, not hers. The thought brought her absolutely no satisfaction.

"I am an old man." Jason's voice took on a whiny note when Ginny remained silent. "I want my grandson here with me. I can tell everyone that it was really me that you had an affair with, and you decided to return my son to me. I'll adopt him, and Lydia will never know what you did to my son's honor."

Ginny was momentarily speechless at the sheer arrogance of the plan, and then a blaze of anger fired through her, loosening her tongue.

"Having seen the job you did raising Creon, I wouldn't trust you with the care of a hamster!"

"Did I forget to mention that I have decided to pay you a hundred thousand dollars to compensate you for any inconvenience this has caused you?" Jason sneered.

A red haze of rage seemed to blur Ginny's vision as she remembered Beth's unshakable faith that Creon hadn't really abandoned her and her inconsolable grief when he had died. And Jason actually thought that money would compensate Beth for the hell that Creon had put her through?

Ginny wanted to grab Jason around his skinny little neck and shake him senseless. She wanted to make him suffer like Beth had suffered. But even as she acknowledged the emotion, she knew it was hopeless. She couldn't change Jason Papas. He was mired so deeply in his prejudices and self-conceit that nothing short of an encounter with the Almighty was going to pry him loose. All Ginny could do at this point was to try to protect Beth and Damon from him.

"You've already ruined Creon. You won't get the chance with his son." Ginny spun on her heel and marched toward the door.

"Don't you dare leave! I haven't finished with you yet," Jason yelled after her.

Ginny paused in the doorway and turned. She supposed she ought to feel sorry for him. He'd lost his son and, if Beth listened to her, he'd never see his grandson, but Ginny found it impossible to pity him. Even faced with that loss, Jason wasn't willing to be reasonable. Bullying seemed to be the only way he knew to interact with people.

"But I've more than finished with you," she said and left the study.

Her shaky legs carried her back through the living room,

and she walked out onto the balcony wanting a breath of
fresh air, even if it was heavily tainted with pollution. Col-
lapsing onto a lounger, Ginny pressed her trembling fingers
against her forehead to try to stop Jason's words from re-
playing in her mind, but the knowledge that Philip had
conspired with that deceitful old man to try to take Damon
from her wouldn't be banished. Philip actually thought that
she could be bought off with money.

It shouldn't have come as a surprise to her, she conceded.
Philip had been conspiring with Jason from the first. He'd
never made any secret of where his sympathies lay.

But even so, the thought that Philip believed that she
could be bought off with money hurt far more than any of
Jason's slurs. It hurt because she didn't care about Jason,
but she loved Philip. The thought hit her with the force of
a blow, causing the blood to drain from her face leaving
her deathly pale.

How could she be in love with Philip Lysander? she
demanded of her reeling mind. When had she fallen in love
with him? Ginny tried to pinpoint the moment in the hope
of neutralizing the feeling. She hadn't loved him in the
beginning. She'd been fascinated by him physically. Then
intrigued by his keen mind, but it hadn't been love.

Ginny sighed in despair, knowing that when and why
weren't important. What was important now was how was
she going to deal with it. She caught her quivering lower
lip between her teeth. Falling in love with unsuitable men
seemed to be a family failing. But as she'd told Beth, no
one had ever died from a broken heart.

The knowledge brought her no more comfort than it had
Beth. But unlike Beth, she was a lot stronger both physically and emotionally, she assured herself. Strong enough
to act instead of dithering. And the only action that made
any sense at this point was to leave Greece. Now. Before

Philip came back and tried to convince her to give Damon away. She couldn't bear to deal with his betrayal face-to-face. It was hard enough to deal with it from a distance.

"I always find a glass of wine helpful after a session with Jason." Lydia's voice came from the open balcony door, and Ginny reluctantly turned to her.

"I don't think the whole bottle would help. Lydia, something has come up, and I have to go home. Today," Ginny added, and the word seemed to echo through her mind like a dirge.

Lydia blinked. "But you cannot!

"At least wait a few days," Lydia pleaded. "Steward called while you were out, and he wants to take you and me to dinner."

Ginny studied Lydia's apprehensive features, having no trouble reading her thoughts. Much as Lydia wanted to go out with Steward, she was afraid to oppose Philip on her own.

Ginny stared blankly down at her yellow dress, at a brown spot that she'd picked up while sightseeing, and tried to think. She had no intention of telling Lydia what she should do about Steward, but before Lydia wasted any more time as a grieving widow, she had a right to know what the husband she was grieving for had really been like.

"Lydia..." Ginny scrambled for a gentle way to put it, and when she couldn't find one, simply blurted it out. "Damon isn't Philip's son—he's Creon's. But I had no idea that Creon was married."

"So that was it," Lydia said slowly. "I wondered why Philip brought you to Jason's villa, and what Jason's interest in the whole thing was."

"You don't seem very surprised," Ginny said tentatively.

Lydia shrugged. "Creon was ever one to fool around. I

found that on our honeymoon. But you are not at all like his normal women."

Ginny gulped, having the feeling that she'd completely lost control of the situation. "I'm not?"

Lydia shook her head. "You are much too strong-willed. Creon liked beautiful women who weren't very experienced."

Because if they had any experience they'd realize what a loser he was. Ginny finished the thought in her own mind. For a brief moment, she debated telling Lydia that she wasn't really Damon's mother, that Beth was. But she finally decided that she'd already said enough. Let Beth decide if she wanted to tell Creon's family the truth.

"Why didn't you tell Philip what Creon was like?" Ginny asked curiously.

Lydia sighed. "How would that have helped? I could not divorce him because of the girls. I might have lost them. At least, part of the time. And nothing Philip could have said to Creon would have made any difference."

"Probably not," Ginny agreed soberly. Creon had been so thoroughly spoiled by Jason that he had been incapable of seeing people as anything other than objects to be used for his own pleasures. And now it was up to her to remove Damon before Jason tried something like spiriting him away somewhere.

Nine

"If you'd like to board now, madam, you'll be able to settle the baby before the rest of the passengers get on." The stewardess gave Ginny a bright, professional smile.

No, I would not like to board now, Ginny thought, clenching her teeth against the pain that threatened to overwhelm her. The last thing she wanted to do was to get on a plane and fly away from Philip. Even knowing that everything they had shared had been tainted by his conspiring with Jason didn't make any difference to how she felt about him. She still loved him. Still wanted to be close to him. Still wanted to cherish him, both physically and mentally.

"Madam?" the stewardess persisted. "Is something wrong?"

"No." Ginny forced the word out as she got to her feet and followed the stewardess into the plane. She had to go before Jason got the idea of trying to get custody of Damon through the Greek courts. While she knew that in such a situation no American court would ever take Damon away from his mother, she couldn't take the risk of what a Greek court might do. Losing Damon, even temporarily, would be a devastating blow to Beth. One she might well not be able to absorb in her present state of mind.

So you fell in love with a louse. So what? Ginny swallowed the tears clogging the back of her throat as she buckled Damon's car seat into the airline seat. The problem was, she couldn't really blame Philip. Not really. He hadn't tricked her into bed. He hadn't had to. The humiliating knowledge added to her sense of despair. She'd been only too eager to make love to him. To rationalize her desires when in her heart she had known better. Known that Philip's loyalties had long since been given elsewhere.

And even if they hadn't been, she'd seen plenty of evidence that Philip subscribed to an archaic set of rules about choosing a wife. When he looked for a permanent relationship with a woman, he'd look among his own social class. He'd pick a meek, self-effacing soul like Lydia who couldn't say boo to a goose.

And he'd live unhappily ever after, Ginny thought miserably. Philip would be bored out of his skull, married to a woman like that.

Ginny finally managed to get Damon safely buckled in and sank down into her own seat. Leaning her head back, she closed her eyes. It would be easier once she was back home among familiar surroundings. She clung to the thought. In New York everything wouldn't remind her of Philip. There she could bury herself in work and not allow herself time to brood over what might have been. By next week, she'd probably wonder why she'd been so upset about leaving Philip, she assured herself, trying hard to believe it.

* * *

Philip shoved open the door to his apartment, and his gaze swept the living room. It was empty. He strode across the room to check the balcony, hoping Ginny wasn't out somewhere. He wanted to see her. He needed to see her. The only thing that had kept him from losing his temper during the day's seemingly interminable labor negotiations had been the thought that once he got home, he could take Ginny in his arms and forget all the day's aggravations in the joy of making love to her. And, afterward, he could hold her close and talk to her. Tell her all about the blind fools he was having to deal with.

To his disappointment only Lydia was there, feeding Jasmine.

"Where's Ginny?" Philip demanded impatiently.

Lydia blinked, startled by his sudden appearance. She peered up at him, trying to decide what to say. Despite what Ginny had said, Lydia didn't think Philip was going to be happy that she'd left. Damon might not have been his, but she'd seen him holding the boy and it was obvious that he cared for him. And as for Ginny herself... Lydia sighed. No man had ever looked at her with that combination of interest and lust in her life. Maybe it would be better to lead up to the news gradually, she finally decided.

"I know about Creon," Lydia said.

"Know what about Creon?" Philip asked cautiously.

"That Damon is his son."

"She shouldn't have told you," he muttered, annoyed that Ginny had disobeyed him, but not really surprised. "There was no reason for you to know, even if it turns out to be true."

Taking a deep breath, Lydia said, "Philip, you are the best brother anyone could ever have, but Ginny is right. This is my life. I have to make my own decisions."

Philip's instinctive reaction was an emphatic denial.

Lydia was too vulnerable, too inexperienced in the ways of the world to know all its pitfalls. But on the heels of that feeling came a trickle of relief. Relief that he was no longer the one responsible for Lydia's happiness. And that made him feel guilty. As if he were too selfish to make the effort to protect his sister.

"Does your sudden revelation have to do with that artist?" he asked suspiciously.

Lydia nervously smoothed the edge of Jasmine's dress. It had taken all of her small store of courage to say what she had. She wasn't sure she could sustain the effort if Philip persisted in arguing. Somehow she had to make him understand how important this was to her.

"In a way. Seeing Steward again forced me out of the rut I was in. Or maybe Ginny forced me out. I do not know. All I know is that I want to be able to explore how I feel, and then to make my own decisions based on what I think is best for me. Not to meekly fall in with what someone else decides is best for me."

Philip heard the hint of determination or desperation—he wasn't sure which—in her voice and realized that his sister had changed. Somehow Ginny had given Lydia the courage to at least attempt to take charge of her own life. Which was hardly surprising, he thought ruefully. Knowing Ginny had made him feel differently about a lot of things, too.

"Will you at least listen to advice?" he asked, not quite ready to agree to letting her go it entirely on her own.

Lydia smiled at him. "If you will agree to let me ignore it."

He smiled back. "I'll try, but—"

"There you are!" Jason's harsh voice ripped through their accord.

Philip swung around in surprise. What was Jason doing

here? He didn't feel up to dealing with Jason's ill humor at the moment. He had too much of his own to work off.

"Why are you in Athens?" Philip asked.

"I got the report from that lab this morning, and I came directly to see that woman," Jason said.

"It was a match?" Philip's disappointment was an almost tangible weight on his shoulders. He hadn't wanted the boy to be Creon's. And not just because of Lydia's feelings, he conceded. He had wanted to be the one to provide for Ginny and the boy. He had wanted her to depend on him, not on Jason.

"Yes," Jason said. "So I told her."

Philip winced. He could imagine what Ginny's reaction to their having gone behind her back like that had been.

"But she already knew that Creon was Damon's father," Lydia said softly.

Jason stared at his daughter-in-law, for once shocked into silence by the fact that Lydia knew what they'd been so careful to keep hidden.

"What did Ginny say?" Philip tried to hurry Jason up.

"Oh, she pretended to be outraged when I said I intended to raise the boy myself, but I've no doubt that it was simply that she didn't think I offered her enough money."

Incredulous anger spilled through Philip. Jason had actually offered Ginny money for her son? Was he an idiot? Anyone could see she loved the boy.

"I want you to tell her that I'm not going to give her one penny more," Jason ordered him. "I want my grandson."

"No," Philip said flatly.

"No?" Jason bellowed, and Jasmine began to cry.

Typically, Jason ignored his granddaughter.

"No," Philip repeated. He didn't give a damn what Jason wanted. It was what Ginny wanted that mattered. "The boy should stay with his mother, and I intend to tell her that."

"Where is she?" Philip turned to Lydia.

Lydia took a deep breath and blurted out, "She left."

"With my grandson?" Jason yelled.

"With her son," Lydia muttered, gently bouncing Jasmine in an attempt to soothe her frightened crying.

Philip stared blankly into Lydia's sympathetic features as a feeling of dread spread through him, fogging his mind and twisting his guts into painful knots. Ginny couldn't have left him. Not without a word. Not after what they'd shared.

"How dare she—" Jason began, but Philip impatiently cut through his bluster.

"Where did she go?"

"Home to New York," Lydia told him. "All I know for certain is that she went into the study with Jason and came out angry. Very angry. She packed up her things and left for the airport."

"Did she have a return ticket?" Philip demanded.

Lydia shrugged. "She did not say, and I did not think to ask."

Philip frantically tried to think. Ginny had obviously left in response to what Jason had said. Which probably meant that she didn't have a reserved seat. With the tourist season in full swing, it was possible that she hadn't been able to get a ticket right away. A sudden flare of hope shot through him. Maybe she was still sitting in the airport, waiting for a seat.

Hastily he turned toward the door. If he was lucky, perhaps he could catch her before she left, and make her understand that taking the boy away from her hadn't been his idea, even if he did have to take the blame for the blood tests.

"Where are you going?" Jason demanded.

"To see if I can catch her before she gets on a plane," Philip threw over his shoulder. "And it would be best if you weren't here when we get back, since she clearly is none too pleased with you at the moment."

Philip hurriedly left the apartment, ignoring Jason's sputters. He still felt that Jason had a right to be involved in his grandson's life, but not to the extent of excluding Ginny. Jason was going to have to learn that Ginny's wishes for the boy came first. And there was no time like the present for him to learn it.

It seemed to take Philip forever to get to the airport through the congested evening traffic. And the longer it took, the more desperate he felt. As if something infinitely precious were slipping away from him.

Finally he managed to reach the airport and, leaving his car in a tow-away zone, sprinted into the terminal. A thorough check of the waiting areas finally convinced him that, contrary to his hopes, Ginny wasn't there.

Leaning against a column, he tried to think. It was difficult. There were too many unanswered questions swirling through his mind, distracting him.

How could Ginny have left him? How could she have betrayed him like this? Didn't she trust him to protect the boy from Jason's machinations? Or didn't she care? The sudden thought hit him with the force of a blow, and he felt dizzy. Taking a deep breath, he forced the thought to the back of his mind. There was no use speculating why Ginny had done what she'd done. The only one who could tell him was Ginny, and she couldn't do that until after he caught up with her.

It took him almost an hour to find which airline she'd used. Despite the fact that he wanted nothing so much as to book another flight for himself, he knew he couldn't. He had to stay and settle the labor problem. If he were to suddenly leave the country, the union would undoubtedly decide that it was a stalling tactic on management's part, and they'd suspend talks. And if they did that, a lot of people would be thrown out of work. People who didn't have the financial wherewithal to absorb the loss of their paychecks.

Philip clenched his teeth in frustration at the seemingly endless responsibilities that hemmed him in.

But even if he couldn't go to her immediately, he could call her once she got back to New York and tell her... Tell her what? he wondered as he headed to his car. What could he say to her? And that was assuming that she'd even talk to him. A sinking feeling dropped through his stomach. She might simply hang up on him. It all depended on how much she thought he was involved in the old man's plans.

Philip climbed into his car and shot away from the curb. She probably thought he was involved up to his neck, and not without some justification, he conceded.

He felt an unaccustomed shiver of uncertainty. Should he call her the minute she arrived in New York or should he give her a few days to calm down?

Worrying about how to handle Ginny's possible reactions caused him to lie awake most of the night. He found it vaguely frightening just how much he missed her. Logically, it made no sense. He hadn't known her long enough to miss her that badly, but he still did.

Shortly after dawn, he gave up all pretense of trying to sleep and called the airline to check that her flight had landed safely. To his relief, it had. Ginny was safely home.

Philip grimaced as he headed for the shower. He couldn't believe how much he missed her. He felt as if something vital had gone out of his life. He even missed the boy. An unconscious smile curved his lips. Damon was a good little kid with a lot of potential. Anyone could see that. He'd make an excellent older brother. Philip's body clenched in reaction to the thought of Ginny having more children. Having his children.

He stepped into the shower and turned the water on, not noticing its chill temperature. He was too caught up in the thought of Ginny pregnant. Of getting Ginny pregnant.

Absently he began to rub soapy lather over his wet skin as he tried to sort out exactly how he felt about her. He couldn't. It was all a jumble. In some ways, she wasn't at all the kind of woman he ever expected to want to marry. For one thing, she didn't come from his social background. But then, Creon had been Lydia's social peer, and look at what a disaster that marriage had been. His fingers unconsciously tightened around the bar of soap he was holding, causing tiny white bubbles to squeeze between his tanned fingers.

Creon was dead, Philip reminded himself. Whatever his faults had been as a husband, he'd more than paid for them. Lydia was free of him. He frowned thoughtfully. And in a strange way, Creon's death had freed him, too. Freed him from the impossible task of trying to assure Lydia's happiness. All he had to worry about now was his own happiness. And Ginny was firmly at the center of it.

Did he love her? Philip held his aching head under the spray, trying to clear his muddled thoughts. He didn't know. He wasn't even sure exactly what love was. The emotion that poets and romantics were forever babbling about didn't describe the way he felt about Ginny. He had no urge to put her on a pedestal and worship her. He wanted to pull her into his bed and make love to her.

But what he felt was far more than simply lust, he conceded. He liked Ginny. Liked her sense of humor and her compassion for Lydia. He liked the way she was willing to

fight for her son. And he liked her intelligence. Her sharp
mind was one of the things that made her so unique. Because after the fantastic sex was over, he could talk to her.
Really talk to her about ideas and concepts instead of just
people, which was all the daughters and the sisters of his
business acquaintances seemed to talk about.

She didn't always agree with him, but at least she didn't
agree with him for a reason. He smiled. One that she had
no hesitation about voicing. In fact, Ginny was the only
woman he knew who was more than willing to argue with
him, and he found it exhilarating.

Love, he finally decided. He loved Ginny Alton, and he
wanted to marry her.

But would she want to marry him? He stepped out of
the shower and began to absently dry himself. A coldness
that had nothing to do with the air temperature feathered
over him, raising goose bumps as it went. If Ginny had
wanted to marry him, wouldn't she have stayed here in
Athens and tried to solidify her position in his bed?
Wouldn't she have tried to get him to talk Jason out of his
idiotic notion of adopting Damon?

Philip sighed. He didn't know. That was one of the problems with his relationship with Ginny. There were far too
many things about her that he didn't know. And some of
the things he did know didn't add up.

Dropping his wet towel on the ceramic floor, he trailed
out of the bathroom to get dressed. Her coming to Greece
to ask Jason for money was high on that list. It simply
didn't fit her very independent personality. His reading of
her character would have been that she would have con-
signed Creon to the devil and gotten on with raising her
son. Which was exactly what she had done for four months.
So why had she suddenly decided to demand money?

Philip yanked on his briefs in frustration. It didn't make

any sense to him, but he didn't doubt for a moment that it did to Ginny. She was a very logical person. Hopefully, logical enough to see the wisdom of marrying him. His eyes strayed to the phone, and he shuddered.

Ginny might be logical, but she could also be very emotional at times, and he wasn't sure whether a proposal from him would appeal to her logical side or her emotional side. Either way, it was going to be tricky.

He pulled a T-shirt over his head. Too tricky to ask her over the phone to marry him. She could so easily hang up on him, he decided. He should propose to her in person. Then he could convince her that marrying him would be the best thing she could do. Then he could assure her that he was willing to accept Damon as his son.

And he couldn't ask her in person until he could somehow end the labor dispute. But maybe it was for the best. If she didn't hear from him for a few days, it would give her time to realize she missed him. Or to realize that she didn't miss him. He swallowed as his stomach churned nervously. It would be all right, he tried to convince himself. Ginny would miss him. He refused to even consider the alternative.

What was she doing now? he wondered as he slipped into a white shirt. Was she staring around her empty apartment and missing him?

"Ginny! You're back!" Beth grabbed Damon's car seat out of Ginny's arms and rained kisses down on the baby's sleepy face. Damon gurgled happily at her.

Ginny closed the apartment door behind her and studied Beth.

"You look good," Ginny said.

Beth looked up from Damon and gave Ginny a happy smile. "I feel it, too. The doctor says I'm doing even better

than he'd hoped. And now that I've got Damon back..."
She cuddled him close to her.

Ginny dropped Damon's diaper bag on the floor and sank
wearily onto the sofa. Closing her eyes, she tried to draw
on the peace of her apartment and her love for Beth to fill
the vast empty space inside her. It didn't work. She still
felt as if her heart had been ripped out, and she was hem-
orrhaging her life's force away. And what was worse was
she didn't much care. Without Philip, her life didn't seem
to have any purpose.

"Bad flight?" Beth asked sympathetically.

Ginny just nodded. Much as she wanted to burst into
tears, she knew she couldn't. Beth was barely strong
enough to cope with her own problems, let alone hers.

"You came back rather suddenly," Beth said. "Didn't
Mr. Papas believe that Damon was his grandson?"

"Not at first, but then he had some blood tests run. Without my knowledge." Ginny's voice sharpened in remembered outrage. "At any rate, the tests proved to Jason's
satisfaction that Damon was Creon's."

"So he's acknowledged Damon?" Beth asked eagerly.

Ginny took a deep breath, reminded herself yet again that
Beth was an adult who deserved to know of any problems
that might have to be faced and said, "He wants to adopt
Damon and raise him himself."

"What!" Beth's arms tightened convulsively around Damon, who squeaked indignantly. "Sorry, angel." Beth
rocked him, her gentle motion in sharp contrast to her mil-
itant expression.

"I told him what he could do with his idea and hopped
the first plane out of Greece," Ginny assured her.

"Thank goodness for that." Beth's tense features relaxed
slightly. "Creon's father doesn't sound as if he improves
on longer acquaintance."

"That's the understatement of the year," Ginny muttered, trying to decide how best to tell Beth about Lydia. With Jason wanting to get his hands on Damon, it was simply a matter of time until all the sordid details came out. Far better that Beth find out from her now so that she could build her defenses.

Deciding that there was no good way to break that kind of news, Ginny said, "Beth, Creon had a wife back in Greece. A wife of seven years and three little girls."

Beth stared at her, her face going chalk white. "A wife?" she whispered.

Ginny nodded unhappily. "I'm sorry."

"So that's why he couldn't marry me. It explains so much. It was probably an arranged marriage that he'd been forced into, and he was trying to find an honorable way out, and he didn't tell me for fear I wouldn't wait for him."

But he wasn't so honorable that he wasn't willing to indulge in an affair with you, Ginny thought cynically, but she didn't say it. She'd told Beth the truth as she knew it. How Beth chose to interpret it was her business.

Tiredly Ginny got to her feet. "It's all history now. At the moment all I want is a hot shower and a long nap."

"Ginny." Beth's voice stopped her as she headed toward the bedroom. "Thanks for everything."

"My pleasure." Ginny gave Beth what she hoped would pass for a sincere smile. At the moment, she felt as if she'd never smile convincingly again.

Time. She repeated the old bromide for surviving a love affair gone bad. All she needed was time.

As a theory it sounded good, but in practical terms it didn't show the slightest sign of working. Ginny simply couldn't put Philip out of her mind. His image was firmly embedded in the deepest recesses of who and what she was. Everything she saw and touched reminded her of Philip.

Finally, after two days of moping around the apartment and trying to pretend that everything was fine, Ginny plunged back into her normal, frantic work schedule, hoping that by concentrating on developing financial markets she'd be able to forget her own emotional problems.

It didn't work. Thoughts of Philip refused to be banished. They played havoc with her concentration, and she found herself making careless, embarrassing mistakes.

To make matters worse, she was having trouble sleeping, and she had absolutely no desire to eat. All she wanted to do was to withdraw into her thoughts of Philip. To replay in her mind everything he had ever said. Every kiss they'd ever shared. And especially to replay the wonder of their lovemaking.

It was a week later, when she stepped on her bathroom scale and found she'd lost twelve pounds, that Ginny realized that somehow she was going to have to come to grips with the fact that she loved a man who didn't love her.

And she would. A momentary flash of her normal independence surfaced through her pain. Philip was safely in Greece, and sooner or later she'd forget him. She sniffed unhappily. Provided she lived long enough.

"I hope you enjoyed your flight with us, sir, and enjoy your stay in America," the steward said to Philip as he hurried to be the first one off the plane. Philip never even heard him. His whole focus was on getting to Ginny as quickly as possible. He had to see her. To touch her. To make love to her. He felt as if he'd never be whole again until he could do that.

If she refused to see him... A shudder shook his powerful frame. He didn't know what he'd do if she wouldn't talk to him. Probably camp on her doorstep and go quietly insane.

An hour later, a taxi delivered him to Ginny's address, which he'd gotten from Jason. Climbing out of the cab, he stared up at the gray limestone building, searching the third floor where her apartment was, in the hopes of catching a glimpse of her in a window. Not surprisingly, he didn't, and he hurried into the lobby.

He was staring at the call boxes for the various apartments, trying to figure out how he could get upstairs without letting her know he was here, when someone spoke to him.

"Are you looking for someone?"

Philip turned to find a stylishly dressed, elderly woman smiling at him.

"I was about to go upstairs when I realized that I'd forgotten my key," he lied.

The woman shook her head in sympathy. "My dear husband could never remember his key, either." She inserted her own key in the security device beside the elevator. "What floor are you on?"

"Three." Philip said, having trouble concentrating on anything other than the fact that Ginny was here in this building and soon he'd be seeing her.

His body clenched nervously as the elevator doors opened on three. Taking a deep breath, he hurried down the hall toward Ginny's apartment, not even hearing the old woman's cheerful goodbye from the elevator. He felt dizzy and faintly nauseous. He wanted Ginny so much, and if she didn't want him... He swallowed on the bitter taste in his mouth, trying not to dwell on the worst-case scenario.

Locating Ginny's apartment halfway down the hall, he rapped sharply on the door. Nothing happened. He was about to knock again when the door suddenly opened.

Philip instinctively took a step forward and then stopped when he realized that the woman standing there wasn't

Ginny. He frowned in confusion. She looked a lot like Ginny. Sort of like a watercolor copy of a vivid oil. But she wasn't Ginny. Even if she was holding Damon, his confused mind registered.

"Erpet!" Damon burbled happily at him, and Philip absently tickled the baby's cheek.

"Who are you?" Philip shot the question at the strange woman.

Beth's eyes narrowed speculatively as she studied the stranger in front of her. He looked Greek and sounded British and, if the hand-tailored suit and the wafer-thin watch she could see on his wrist were any indication, he was rich. She noted the lines around his tightly compressed lips. He also appeared to be under some sort of strain.

She glanced down at Damon who was happily blowing bubbles at the man. If Damon knew him, then he had to be someone Ginny knew. Probably someone Ginny had met in Greece.

"Ginny is at work," Beth said slowly. "I'm her cousin Beth, and this is—"

"I know who the boy is. He's very promising."

Promising? Beth examined his description and found it curious. And somehow touching.

"And you are?" Beth persisted.

"Philip Lysander. Where does Ginny work?"

Beth briefly debated the wisdom of telling him and finally decided that if Ginny didn't want to see him, she was quite capable of getting rid of him. Beth gave him the address of Wintons.

Philip absently patted Damon on the head, nodded to Beth and hurried back down the hall. Beth watched him disappear into the elevator, wondering if he was the reason Ginny had seemed so preoccupied since she'd come back from Greece.

Philip hailed a cab outside the apartment building and gave Ginny's work address to the driver, assuming that it was the school where Ginny taught. To his surprise, the cabdriver delivered him to a high-rise office building. Maybe Wintons was a private kindergarten that cared for the children of the building's workers.

Going inside, he checked the directory and discovered that it wasn't a school at all. Wintons was an investment firm. Philip frowned. If Ginny worked for an investment company, that would explain how she had known so much about that Mexican company. But it didn't explain why she would have told Jason that she was a kindergarten teacher.

One more thing about Ginny that didn't add up. But at the moment, he didn't care. All he cared about was that he was about to see Ginny. Finally. A surge of anticipation twisted his nerves.

He got into the elevator as the doors opened and hastily punched the button for the eighth floor. Wintons was immediately to the right of the elevator.

Opening the door, he stepped into a luxurious reception area that radiated taste and competence. It seemed the perfect background for Ginny.

"May I help you, sir?" The receptionist gave him a bright smile.

"I'm here to see Miss Alton." Philip never even noticed the interest in her eyes.

"She's the third door on the right down that hallway." The woman pointed to the left. "Whom should I tell her is here?"

Philip ignored her. Hurrying down the hall, he stopped in front of the heavy oak door with Ginny's name on it. He reached out and lightly traced his finger over the brass engraving, delighting in the sensation of touching something that was hers.

Mentally bracing himself, he knocked on the door.

Ginny glanced up at the sound.

"Come in," she called, hoping it wasn't a colleague wanting to gossip. The effort to be friendly was more than she could muster at the moment.

Her eyes widened and a roaring sound filled her ears as she saw Philip in the doorway.

"Philip?" she whispered, afraid to believe it was really him and not a figment of her tortured imagination.

He stepped inside and closed the door behind him. "You look like hell!" he said, shocked at her pale face.

Ginny felt a glorious sense of exhilaration fill her at his description. It really was Philip! She didn't know why he was here or what he wanted, and she didn't care. It was enough that she was able to stare at his beloved features.

"And you've lost weight!" he added. "And why did you tell Jason you were a kindergarten teacher?"

Ginny let the vibrant sound of his voice pour through her. Just being in the same room with him made her feel alive. Charged with energy.

"You aren't answering me!"

Ginny stared at him as she suddenly realized something strange. She'd rather be yelled at by Philip than made love to by anyone else.

"Well?" he demanded.

Ginny shook herself free of her thoughts as she tried to decide what to say. He was going to be livid when he found out that she'd told Lydia about Damon. But she wanted that out of the way first.

Bracing herself, she said, "I told Lydia the truth about Damon."

To her surprise, he merely waved his hand as if brushing away something of little consequence.

"She already told me. Now suppose you tell me why

you ran away like that without even talking to me? You knew that I was having labor problems and wouldn't be able to follow you.''

Ginny instinctively responded to the hurt she could hear in his voice. ''I couldn't let Jason have Damon. And I was afraid that you'd try to convince me what a great idea it was.''

''It isn't, and I wouldn't,'' Philip said succinctly ''You're the boy's mother. A child belongs with its mother.''

''About Damon...'' she started to say.

Philip sat down on the edge of her desk, his muscular thigh scant inches from her bare forearm. Ginny licked her dry lips as the warmth of his body washed over her. A throbbing sparked to life deep in her abdomen as she remembered how that warmth had felt against her naked body.

With a monumental effort, she forced herself to concentrate on explanations. ''He isn't.''

''He isn't what?'' Philip lightly ran the tip of his forefinger down over her cheek.

Ginny shuddered as a wave of longing poured through her, further distracting her. It was getting harder and harder to maintain her train of thought. Her eyelids felt weighted, and it was so much trouble to keep them open.

''Damon isn't my son,'' she mumbled.

''What!''

Philip's sharp exclamation jerked her gaze up. He was staring at her with an expression she found unnerving.

''Damon is my cousin Beth's child.'' She forced herself to complete the explanation.

Philip stared blankly at Ginny, trying to grasp what she was saying. One fact seemed to burn into his mind.

''You lied to me!''

Ginny winced. "Kind of, but—"

"Kind of! You told me you were a kindergarten teacher. You aren't. You told me you were Damon's mother. You aren't."

What else had she lied about? The appalling fear surfaced through his sense of outrage. Had her wholehearted response to his lovemaking been a lie, too? A numbing sensation seeped through him, freezing his chaotic emotions into a solid block of anger. An anger fueled by his fear and uncertainty.

"But I didn't lie to *you!*" Ginny desperately tried to make him understand. To break through the coldness she could see glazing his eyes. His rigid expression made her feel chilled to the very depths of her being. As if she were looking into her own bleak, desolate future.

"Like hell you didn't lie to me!" His bitter tone tore at Ginny's already ragged composure.

"I mean, I didn't set out to lie to you personally. I didn't even know you existed when I went to Greece."

"But you still lied!" Philip couldn't seem to get past that one point because it raised the horrible specter that everything else they'd shared had been a lie.

"All right, have it your way! I lied!" Ginny shot back, beginning to lose her temper. "I lied to protect my cousin. I lied to try to save her more pain from Jason Papas. I lied out of loyalty to my family and, considering the fact that the first thing you said to me was that I had to lie about who Damon's father was, your moral outrage rings a little false, my friend!"

"That's different! I was only trying to..." His voice trailed off under Ginny's scornful eyes.

He jumped as the phone on her desk suddenly rang, and Ginny automatically answered it.

Jerkily Philip got to his feet and wandered over to the

window. Twitching aside the curtain he stared down at the busy street far below and tried to think. To consider Ginny's charade impersonally. It was impossible. He couldn't think of anything that applied to Ginny in impersonal terms.

But she was right about one thing, he conceded. He had been willing to lie to protect his sister, so he could hardly complain that Ginny had used the same tactics on him in her defense of her cousin. In fact, her unwavering loyalty to her family was a very Greek trait. An admirable trait that he and their children would benefit from. Always provided he could convince her to marry him. Although...

He frowned as something suddenly occurred to him. If Ginny had lied about being Damon's mother, that meant that she hadn't had an affair with Creon. It was her cousin who had been Creon's lover. An overwhelming feeling of relief washed through him, seeming to take a great weight with it as it ebbed. A weight that he hadn't fully realized he'd carried until it was gone.

Philip shifted uneasily. He might feel better about the whole situation, but how did Ginny feel? He wanted her so much, and if she didn't want him...

"Now, where were we in the catalog of abuse you were heaping on me?" Ginny's voice yanked him out of the labyrinth of his self-doubt.

Philip stared at her exasperated features, feeling a longing for her that seemed to have no boundaries. Even if she rejected his proposal, he still had to try. But first he ought to try to soothe her ruffled temper, he decided.

"I'm sorry," he offered hopefully.

"Oh? For which particular insult are you sorry?"

"Any, all," he muttered. Shoving his fingers through his hair, he took a deep breath and blurted out, "Marry me." Then, afraid that he might have sounded too abrupt, added, "Please."

Ginny froze as his words seemed to echo around the room. She tilted her head back and stared into his tense features, trying to figure out if she had really heard what she thought she'd heard or if her mind were playing tricks on her.

"I can easily shift the base of my operations from London to New York so that you can continue to work here," Philip coaxed when she just sat there staring at him in utter silence.

Ginny suddenly realized that her light-headedness was caused by the fact that she wasn't breathing. Hurriedly gulping in air, she tried to figure out what was going on. She couldn't. His proposal didn't make any sense. He had been very clear about the qualities he expected to get in a wife, and she didn't have any of them. Was this some kind of cruel joke? A payback for having told Lydia about Damon?

Ginny stared into his night-dark eyes, not understanding the emotions she saw seething in them. No, she quickly rejected the idea. Philip might be aggravating at times, but he was never deliberately cruel. If he asked her to marry him, he meant it.

"Why?" Ginny forced the word out, and then instinctively braced herself for his answer.

"Because I love you, dammit!" he snapped, fear of rejection making him short-tempered.

Ginny gave him a slow, seductive smile as a feeling of utter happiness welled through her. "Oh, that's all right, then. Of course I'll marry you."

"You will?" he asked cautiously.

"Oh, yes." She put her arms around his shoulders and tugged him closer. "Because in case you haven't figured it out yet, I happen to love you to distraction."

* * * * *

SILHOUETTE® *Desire*®

15 YEARS OF GUARANTEED GOOD READING!

Desire has always brought you satisfying novels that let you escape into a world of endless possibilities—with heroines who are in control of their lives and heroes who bring them passionate romance beyond their wildest dreams.

When you pick up a Silhouette Desire, you can be confident that you won't be disappointed. Desire always has six fresh and exciting titles every month by your favorite authors—**Diana Palmer, Ann Major, Dixie Browning, Lass Small and BJ James,** just to name a few. Watch for extraspecial stories by these and other authors in **October, November and December 1997** as we celebrate **Desire's 15th anniversary.**

Indulge yourself with three months of top authors and fabulous reading…we even have a fantastic promotion waiting for you!

Pick up a Silhouette Desire… it's what women want today.

Available at your favorite retail outlet.

SD15YR

Take 4 bestselling love stories FREE

Plus get a FREE surprise gift!

Special Limited-time Offer

Mail to Silhouette Reader Service™

3010 Walden Avenue
P.O. Box 1867
Buffalo, N.Y. 14240-1867

YES! Please send me 4 free Silhouette Desire® novels and my free surprise gift. Then send me 6 brand-new novels every month, which I will receive months before they appear in bookstores. Bill me at the low price of $2.90 each plus 25¢ delivery and applicable sales tax, if any.* That's the complete price and a savings of over 10% off the cover prices—quite a bargain! I understand that accepting the books and gift places me under no obligation ever to buy any books. I can always return a shipment and cancel at any time. Even if I never buy another book from Silhouette, the 4 free books and the surprise gift are mine to keep forever.

225 BPA A3UU

Name   (PLEASE PRINT)

Address   Apt. No.

City   State   Zip

This offer is limited to one order per household and not valid to present Silhouette Desire® subscribers. *Terms and prices are subject to change without notice.
Sales tax applicable in N.Y.

UDES-696   ©1990 Harlequin Enterprises Limited

FANTASTIC NEWS!

For all you devoted Diana Palmer fans
Silhouette Books is pleased to bring you
a brand-new novel and short story by one of the
top ten romance writers in America

"Nobody tops Diana Palmer...I love her stories."
—*New York Times* bestselling author
Jayne Ann Krentz

Diana Palmer has written another thrilling desire.
Man of the Month Ramon Cortero was a talented
surgeon, existing only for his work—until the
night he saved nurse Noreen Kensington's life. But
their stormy past makes this romance a challenge!

THE PATIENT NURSE
Silhouette Desire
October 1997

And in November Diana Palmer adds to the
Long, Tall Texans series with *CHRISTMAS COWBOY*, in
LONE STAR CHRISTMAS, a fabulous new holiday
keepsake collection by talented authors Diana Palmer
and Joan Johnston. Their heroes are seductive,
shameless and irresistible—and these Texans are
experts at sneaking kisses under the mistletoe! So get
ready for a sizzling holiday season....

Only from  Silhouette®

LTTXMAS

Daniel MacGregor is at it again...

New York Times bestselling author

NORA ROBERTS

introduces us to a new generation of MacGregors
as the lovable patriarch of the illustrious MacGregor
clan plays matchmaker again, this time to his three
gorgeous granddaughters in

THE MACGREGOR BRIDES

From Silhouette Books

Don't miss this brand-new continuation of Nora Roberts's
enormously popular *MacGregor* miniseries.

Available November 1997 at your favorite retail outlet.

Look us up on-line at: http://www.romance.net   NRMB-S

COMING THIS OCTOBER 1997 FROM

THREE NEW LOVE STORIES IN ONE VOLUME BY
ONE OF AMERICA'S MOST BELOVED WRITERS

DEBBIE MACOMBER

Three Brides, No Groom

Gretchen, Maddie and Carol—they were three college
friends with plans to become blushing brides. But
even though the caterers were booked, the bouquets
bought and the bridal gowns were ready to wear...the
grooms suddenly got cold feet. And that's when these
three women decided they weren't going to get mad...
they were going to get even!

DON'T MISS THE WARMTH, THE HUMOR...THE
ROMANCE AS ONLY DEBBIE MACOMBER CAN DO!

**AVAILABLE WHEREVER SILHOUETTE BOOKS
ARE SOLD.**

TBNG-S